What
We
Won't Do

What We Won't Do

STORIES

Brock Clarke

Winner of the 2000
Mary McCarthy Prize in Short Fiction
Selected by Mark Richard

Sarabande  Books

LOUISVILLE, KENTUCKY

Managing Editor
Sarabande Books, Inc.
2234 Dundee Road, Suite 200
Louisville, KY 40205

LIBRARY OF CONGRESS CATALOGING-IN-PUBLICATION DATA

Clarke, Brock.
    What we won't do : stories / by Brock Clarke.— 1st ed.
    p.   cm.
    "Winner of the 2000 Mary McCarthy Prize in Short Fiction, selected by Mark Richard."
    Contents: Foreword / by Mark Richard — A widespread, killing frost — Specify the learners — She loved to cook but not like this — The fat — The world dirty, like a heart — What we won't do — The right questions — Compensation — Plowing the secondaries — Accidents — Starving — The reasons — Up north.
    ISBN 1-889330-67-1 (acid-free paper)
    1. United States—Social life and customs—20th century—Fiction. I. Title.

PS3603.L37 W47 2002
813'.6—dc21
2001031087

Cover and text design by Charles Casey Martin

Manufactured in the United States of America
This book is printed on acid-free paper.

Sarabande Books is a nonprofit literary organization.

Funded in part by a grant from the Kentucky Arts Council, a state agency of the Education, Arts, and Humanities Cabinet.

FIRST EDITION

For
Colin, Alonzo, and Quinn

Contents

Acknowledgments

Stories in this collection have previously appeared in the following publications:

"Plowing the Secondaries," *New England Review* (Fall 2001)

"Accidents," *Mississippi Review Web* (Spring 2001)

"She Loved to Cook but Not Like This," *New England Review* (Fall 2000)

"What We Won't Do," *Our Working Lives* (Fall 2000)

"The Fat," *Tatlin's Tower* (Fall 2000)

"The Right Questions," *The Journal* (Winter 1999)

"The World Dirty, Like a Heart," *American Fiction* (Spring 1999)

"Up North," *The South Carolina Review* (Fall 1999)

"Compensation," *New England Review* (Spring 1998)

"A Widespread Killing Frost," *Mississippi Review* (December 1997)

"The Reasons," *American Fiction* (December 1996)

Thanks to Sarah Gorham, Kirby Gann, Nickole Brown, and all the other good folks at Sarabande for their hard work and good humor, and to Mark Richard for saying Yes.

Thanks to Elizabeth Sheinkman, agent extraordinaire.

Thanks also to all those friends—from Breadloaf, Sewanee, Rochester, Clemson, and elsewhere—who read these stories and didn't say they were sorry I'd written them, especially Keith Morris.

Thanks to all the editors of the publications where these stories appeared, and a special thanks to Jodee Stanley Rubins for her huge and tireless support.

And thanks, finally and always, to Lane.

Foreword

What is the significance of hot chicken grease blown from a KFC exhaust fan all over a broken-down station wagon? Can you assign its significance to the rise and ruin of human affections? Would you believe me if I told you the author of this book can and did? What about people who refer to marriage as their Complete Fucking Nightmare? Would you think there was any thing, any way with which they could redeem their vows, or at least the stasis of an armed marital truce? What about Final Failures? Slow Steady Regret? Being Wronged by Life? Are these themes with which you are familiar? Isn't that what fiction is supposed to be? Isn't it an examination of the goddamn misery of our daily lives in all its tedium and struggle and disappointment and loss and trying to find one little glimmer of hope and comfort? Even from a six-pack of cheap beer or a copy of *Chicks with Dicks* or a thawing of a love for a dying parent? How about if you could look at all that, and the absolutely rotten things we do and enjoy doing to ourselves and each other, and laugh out loud at the absurdity and familiarity of it all and be moved, wouldn't that be something? What about a book about low expectations, for crying out loud? What about a book about all the goddamn settling we have to do that tries to snuff us out quietly? Would you like a book that makes you nod knowingly when it says there are only two things true about the matter of settling: NEVER SETTLE and SOMETIMES YOU HAVE TO SETTLE? Wouldn't you just know the problem is not that you don't know *when* to settle, but that you don't know when you already have?

Here it is, this is the book.

You know why I like this book so much? It's disarmingly entertaining, all the trouble the poor bastards are going through answering the questions of What matters? What do I really need—is it work, friends, money a connectiveness to the world? It's subversively pornographic in the most enlightening sense—watching the poor bastards slap their party host's child who calls them an asswipe; listening to them cajole their naked, trash can-bearing fathers out onto the lawn only to heckle; struggling with the murderous arson of Emily Dickenson's house. Seeing the interconnected lives in this little town, you finally have to ask yourself: What exactly is it in MY life that I'm so goddamn afraid of, at the risk of losing faith, hope, and clarity?

Here are the proclamations of the characters within this volume of excellent stories:

I was wrong, but I'm not sorry!
I won't be afraid of this life!
I am glad the elephant killed my son!
I accept the fact that I don't WANT to be a better person!
If only I could repeat sixth grade, my life would be different!

The honesty herein is not the sugarcoated sort, it's the sort that exacts revenge by goading others into doing what we can't or won't do ourselves. And yet there are the consequences, plenty, and they are the mortal kind of crossing boundaries not by sheer conviction, but as in real life, conviction trimmed with recklessness and fueled by an inflated sense of effrontery. You haven't read these stories before, and that's the highest compliment that I can pay them. That and the fact that they made me laugh, out loud, and frightened me a little, and still do.

—*Mark Richard, July 2000*

I'd rather have a wreck than a ship that sails.
Things attach themselves to wrecks.

—Donald Barthelme

What
We
Won't Do

A Widespread Killing Frost

B ad blood down at the VA hospital. Outside we've got a widespread killing frost, and I'm in knots over my Wandering Jews. Inside the cripples are cranking it up on the subject of Jacksonville, Florida.

"I have traveled to Jacksonville twice, without expectation," says one of the old sufferers.

This Young Turk, Thomas, takes on a smug look and superior posture. He should. He claims that the Jacksonville International Airport gives him an absolutely terrific erection.

All the enduring and noble old centurions are set off by this big whopper. They shuffle over and let loose in the name of everything true and reasonable.

"Jacksonville has a passable modern art museum," someone says.

"I am happy to say that Jacksonville is not the state capital," the first old geezer shoots back.

"I couldn't find not a one pinball machine in the whole city," another one says. "Not one pinball player neither. I would've got the high score."

"I've never been to Jacksonville," Thomas tells them. "It's the airport I'm talking about."

"Does it carry *The New York Times?*" I ask.

"I don't think that's it," Thomas says.

"Then maybe it's something in the air," I say.

Thomas fixes me a stare and says, "I tell you true, there is nothing funny about it."

Which is, in fact, the sad truth. This poor man would have us believe he spends his brief adulthood winging around this big old country, rerouting himself past convenience and expense to experience the X-rated pleasures of the Jacksonville International Airport. Then, all he's left with is the story itself, which no one believes but everyone hates him for. There is absolutely nothing funny about it.

Then again, he's no worse off than the rest of the Young Turks, who are in the other corner near-delirious over their validation. They've been chagrinning the government for years about being gassed, poisoned, etc. by the very government itself, while out there in the desert, killing off all those Communistic Muslims. The government has now said, Fine, you've been poisoned. This has set off some fearful celebration in the VA hospital. Someone has smuggled in some beer, someone else cigarettes. One of them has even gone and wrapped himself in the American flag, which he takes off only when his diarrhea, vomiting, vertigo touches off a counter-celebration that makes drapery ill-advised.

The old cripples hem in poor Thomas and pretend disgust or envy or no interest. They are afraid to look at their younger selves. They are also afraid not to look at them. They take their diversionary potshots at North Florida with one rheumy, collective eye toward the future.

Then there's me, the woman who acts just like a lady florist and lady wife should not. I'm supposed to educate them all about plant life.

Well, the theory goes, I asked for it.

This October 15, on his thirtieth birthday, my husband and I went off drunkenly and declared our love in public spaces. We did this in both

New York and Ontario. This was all according to tradition. When we got home, Bobby Candace remembered he was a Catholic.

"I was confirmed in the year 1980," he said to me.

"That's what I thought," I told him and went to sleep. When I woke up ten hours later, he had given up alcohol, alphabetized our records, and murdered all of my plants except for an Easter cactus, which Bobby Candace thought majestic and not a little holy.

"You're looking at a better man," he told me.

"What happened to my plants?" I asked back.

He stood there handsomely and swallowed some important phrase, which I knew would be a quote and heavy with intent. Then he walked away. Through the sliding glass door I could see all my plants laid out in jagged rows on the deck. Some of them were tipped over. Some of them were upright. They were all taken dead by a frost, exposed to the frost itself by the husband who had overnight revised me into an evil and damning influence. I am a florist. I have a degree, and no one can tell me it was constructive criticism. I mean, this wasn't one of your easy orange-killing frosts you get down South. We've got frosts that can kill cattle if they're already a little sickly and not truly loved.

My husband spent the next month convicting me of poisoning him with eight years of middling debauchery untouched by middle-class reserve. Bobby Candace teaches the creative arts part time at the community center, which means he's got a nimble mind and a thesaurus. Once, I got home from my shop and he'd typed up twenty-odd synonyms for the word "repent."

"Hey," I told him. "We've done things but within the law and only with each other. This is love, is it not?"

"You went to the movies without me," he said.

"It never made the papers," I said.

The spouse's soft heart is starved for proof. Instead of answering me, Bobby Candace went and found a picture of me drunk at our wedding, a speeding ticket, and copies of his and my tax returns, which revealed a prejudice toward capital enterprise and against the life of the mind. Then he ran away singing "Sad sad sad."

That night the sky was clear, and the frost inevitable and charismatic in its sensibilities. Science teaches us that so many things can happen on clear nights, and all of them bad. It doesn't need saying, when I got up the next day my replacement plants were dead. Bobby Candace left me a note on the kitchen table that read: "What goes around, comes around." And then: "With love."

Ultimately, I set about to prove his truth. After three nights of trying I finally introduced my van to the brick wall of a fast-food drive thru. When I got in front of the judge, he said, "You were drunk."

"Correct. I was also hungry," I told him.

The judge sentenced me to community service, and sent me home, where Bobby Candace was waiting. "Are you going to jail?" he asked me.

"I am going to the VA hospital," I said. He looked distraught, his good, young soul choking with self-hate, and it pained me to disappoint him. So I wept a little and said: "The judge said I needed to learn something about hurt. He also said I was developing into a bad woman."

"Well," my husband said, "that's true."

Among florists there is no honor, no lack of honor either, nor a fondness for community, rivalry, or the what-alls of advertising. There is no consensus in sexual preference. There is no celebration of sexual difference. There is no sex. There is no hatred or weakness for complimentary manuals with titles like *How to Grow Tulips in Cold Climates* or *Your House and Hanging Plants*. There is hardly anything at all except for the public joy of our vans, and a fair amount of etymology, which is our private ache. The vans are white, tattooed with a rose or sunflower of nuclear proportions. We buy them used and paint them ourselves. We do not lease because of our fear of mileage restrictions. Sometimes we throw those complimentary manuals in the back and drive at unholy speeds around the dirt roads with potholes like bomb craters, listening to the bindings bounce and snap a little musically like bones.

But the etymology tells us how the world works, except when it tells us how it doesn't. There is power in knowing that "philodendron" means "lover of trees," that "rosemary" comes from the Latin meaning "sea dew," and was used in classical days as a symbol of love's truth. There is relief in discovering that "impatiens" has nothing to do with temperament.

There is no relief in the legend of the Wandering Jew, a clinging ivy who in human form mocked old Jesus on the cross without understanding that mocking was criminal, and was thereupon damned by the savior himself to wander the world until kingdom come. Which is when the savior forgives the Jew or does not.

And there is no relief in the story of my husband, who is anxious and philosophical. One night he goes to bed and realizes that he is thirty and has no idea how he got there without resistance or accomplishment. Like most men of thirty, my Bobby Candace is big on reasons. He turns over in bed and locates one. He explodes my drunk sleep into a long, wet history of contagion. I get less moral and less moral, and he feels better all the time. The past becomes the smoke of convenience and vindication. But for me, the past is all terror and clear promise. Our horse is fine feelings and beauty, and I ride it by memory and as a matter of course. I remember that I loved Bobby Candace and that he loved me. Because it happened that way once, I have faith it could happen again.

I keep buying houseplants and leaving them unattended. Bobby Candace keeps killing them. I keep buying more plants. He used to not kill them. I keep hoping he'll remember why.

Regret is at high tide back at the hospital. The inmates are in full remorse, feeling a lot of bad, after feeling a very little bit of good. They have driven Thomas from the rec room. After losing the war of celebration, dying out to fatigue, beer funnels, and uncertainty of purpose and going in drips to their rooms to chew on a future of expiration or endurance, the leftover Young Turks joined the old crew in shaming poor Thomas out of arousal and into a small fury. Finally, he quit the room, his long black hair flapping out behind him with a facility hateful to the cripple in all of us. Now, the rest of them can't figure out why they did what they did. They can't be sure if there is anything real and good left in the world. Those who don't have visible wounds are about to start in on the ostentation of those who do. I stand up and ask them to fix themselves into a circle. This is what all of us want me to say:

Take back your deluxe heart monitors, cable TV, and cheap emotions.

Give me back my husband, my leg, my faith, my life.

What none of us want is the fulfillment of my community service, but I break out my overhead projector and my notes and have at it anyway.

The one thing you don't want to do when teaching veterans about houseplants is to expose them to *terminology*. My lecture on southern exposure and bay windows is a rare hit and I am right in the middle of my spin about *rhizomes, viviparum,* and *propagation* when I notice their look, which amounts to an expression of final terror. They are being invaded by rhetoric. It is Pearl Harbor '41, Saigon '68, Baghdad '91 all over again.

"You're singing to the chorus," one keen old victim finally tells me.

"Praise Jesus," I tell him.

He looks at me for a good while. He has expansive white eyebrows and a kind, attentive gaze. "You're a real character," he says.

"I am a florist accused of moral contamination."

"I am dying," he says.

"Not so you'd notice," I say.

Then, to cheer him up I relay the story of the Saintpaulia. "The Saintpaulia," I say to him, "is otherwise known as the African Violet. The name violet supposedly comes from Io. Io was a Greek maiden whom Zeus changed into a heifer. He was trying to hide her from his wife, who was jealous of Io. Zeus created violets for that girl, to make up for having turned her into a cow."

"And why would he do that?" the old geezer wants to know. "What kind of comfort is that?"

"I have no idea," I say. What I do know is that I am a florist accused of moral contamination, fearful of high cloud ceilings and turncoat husbandry and adjudication. They are soldiers who have to convince the free world of cause, effect, and premeditation before settling down to the satisfaction of being bona fide, lifelong cripples. We are in a concrete box with high windows glazed with night's black and November's deep frost, and I am supposed to learn what it's like to be dead and dying, except that my teachers have no interest in death as a teaching tool and I am a teaching tool, well-versed in the rigors of plant and home life and terrified of all lessons therein and of. We stop talking because none of us can stand to learn one more new thing about this world. Those of us who can cross our legs do; those who can't pretend a lifelong grudge against leg-crossers. We remain like that for a long time. Outside the frost is beginning to work its way into the ground, making the earth crack, seize up, and cleave with the force of the cold as we sit there quietly, very quietly, and with a little hope.

Starving

Two weeks before Thanksgiving, a group of fathers in Little Falls called an emergency meeting and decided, after considerable deliberation, to starve themselves to death. The fathers were all widowers and all of them had sons who, upon reaching the age of forty just a few weeks earlier, became mysteriously and totally dissatisfied with their lives. "What in the hell am I doing?" the sons asked themselves. "I am fucking *better* than this." What *this* was, exactly, the sons could not say, but they were certain of their superiority to it, and so they went about destroying their perfectly good marriages and alienating their young children and wrecking their late-model pickups driving home drunk from the Renaissance and the Happen Inn at two in the morning. In the absolute heat of their self-destruction the sons also quit their jobs at the fiberglass plant and the paper mill and did not stop to consider how they were going to pay their rent, etc. without their seven fifty an hour, plus overtime.

After two months of unemployment and high bachelor hedonism, the sons ran out of money. Thus, broke and ruinously sober, the sons began to realize exactly what they had done and how horrible their lives were likely to be from here on out. So they sucked it up, called their wives, and begged them for forgiveness.

"Ha!" the wives said. The wives had already begun their new lives, and had already begun to like those lives better than their old ones. "Fat chance," the wives said, and then hung up.

And so the sons, having no other option, were forced to move in with their fathers.

Upon moving in with their fathers, the sons' heedless self-destruction turned to aching self-pity. The self-pity was so severe that the sons could bring themselves to do nothing but lie on their fathers' couches and drink their fathers' Utica Club and pollute the houses with their black, self-pitying moods. The moods were so very black that the fathers often walked around their houses in the middle of the day, turning on lights and saying, "*Jesus*, it's dark in here." Then, after their eyes had adjusted to the light, the fathers saw their sons lying on the couch, at the very center of all the darkness. "I feel just *awful*," the sons said. The fathers felt pretty awful themselves and they quickly turned the lights back off so that they wouldn't have to look at their sad-sack sons for one more second than they already had.

Finally, two weeks before Thanksgiving, the fathers decided they couldn't take it anymore, which was when they agreed as a group to starve themselves to death, so as to put themselves out of their misery, and maybe teach their sons a lesson in the bargain.

After they had reached their decision, the fathers went home, leaned over their sons, who were still lying on their couches in positions of perfectly tortured lassitude, and told the sons what they were going to do.

"You're going to starve yourself to *death?*" the sons said.

"Correct," the fathers said.

"Why in the hell would you want to do a thing like that?" the sons asked.

"Because of you," each of the fathers said, because these were the kind of men who could only speak in blunt sentences close to the truth.

"I can't stand it, seeing you mope around the house the way you are. You're making me miserable."

"Dad, be reasonable," each of the sons said. They argued that just because they had made their fathers miserable (they did not deny that they had made their fathers miserable), did not mean that their old men had the right to kill themselves in such a gruesome fashion. After all, the sons said, all children make their parents miserable at one time or another, and wasn't this taking things a bit too far? The fathers didn't pay much attention to this argument at all.

"Save your breath, son," each father said. "My mind is made up. You can be as pathetic as you want to from now on. It doesn't matter to me anymore." The fathers looked down at their sons, their gray impressive eyebrows curling ominously over their rheumy eyes; the fathers fondly ruffled their sons' hair like they had done some twenty years earlier, and then left the room.

The sons, who were as secure in their self-pity as they had previously been in their superiority, calmly picked up their phones and called each other after their fathers had left the room. "Don't worry about it," the sons told each other. After all, they reminded each other, didn't all fathers make grand, apocalyptic threats from time to time? And wasn't it expected that the sons would ignore the threats until they went away? And so, after a brief consultation, the sons concluded that their fathers were bluffing. The sons also concluded that they should remain on the couch as much as humanly possible and drink Utica Club with the lights off and generally stay the course.

The fathers began to starve themselves, as promised. After the first two weeks they began to look very handsome: the fathers lost some of the beer fat around their guts and under their chins, and their cheeks hollowed out some. There was an unusual glow about the fathers as well: their faces were just on the gold side of jaundice. The fathers were so handsome that when they and their sons went to the high school basketball game on Friday night, all the single mothers in town began to buzz around the fathers, asking them if they had been to Florida, had they joined a gym, were they on one of those high-protein diets. The fathers' wives had died only a few years earlier—from brain tumors and multiple sclerosis and from the various misdiagnoses of their country doctors—and so the fathers weren't exactly used to all this female attention. But by the end of the game, they seemed completely at ease with their new status as local sex symbols. As the fathers were leaving the gym, the mothers of the basketball players—who were all divorced and desperate about it, and who all wore too much make-up and tight designer knock-off jeans—put their hands on the fathers' shoulders and whispered: "Looking good."

"Feeling good," the fathers said, in the manner of Humphrey Bogart smooth talking Lauren Bacall, not in the manner of starving, sixty-six-year-old men bantering with the town sluts.

The sons stood transfixed in the high school hall as they watched their fathers' radical transformation. To the sons, it was as if they were witnessing something holy, something very much like a rebirth. Witnessing this act of regeneration, the sons felt a deep, calming sense of satisfaction. It was because of the sons' irresponsible behavior, after all, that their fathers were now so attractive and in such high romantic demand. The sons looked at each other and wiped the back of their hands across their brows in a pantomime of relief: if this was all their fathers' starvation was going to amount to, then they could easily imagine life going on as it was endlessly, and their fathers' starvation would be but a small ripple on the clear lake of their leisurely, self-pitying days.

The sons' good feeling disappeared, however, as their fathers' starvation progressed rapidly over the subsequent weeks. The sons had all surreptitiously purchased copies of the *Merck Manual of Medical Information*, and so they knew what was supposed to happen to their fathers when—that is, if the fathers kept up with their self-starvation, which the sons doubted. But by the time December hit, the fathers lost their glow entirely: their skin became parchmentlike, pale, and very cold; and their hair began to fall out in clumps—the sons would find piles of it in the Berber carpet, on the kitchen counters, on the fathers' pillows. The sons consulted their medical manuals and discovered that these were symptoms of an *advanced* stage of starvation, which meant that the fathers were well ahead of where they were supposed to be. This was just fucking *typical* of the fathers, who had been efficient in everything they had ever done, and it was also typical that they not complain about their condition or ask for help or call attention to themselves in any way. In fact, these were qualities that the sons had always resented in their fathers. The sons had always felt their fathers had set a high standard of steadfastness and self-sufficiency that the sons themselves could never hope to achieve. After they discovered that their fathers starved themselves in much the same manner in which they lived their lives, the sons became infuriated.

"Son of a bitch if they aren't showing us up *again*," the sons told each other on the phone. One of them remembered how his father had roofed an entire barn in just three hours; another said how his father had made half as much money as the son himself had and yet somehow saved twice as much; still another son told about how his father once tore apart and then rebuilt his 1968 Dodge Duster. "I can't even change a tire," the son said. "Son of a *bitch.*"

In this fashion the sons worked themselves into a high pitch of resentment and became even more intransigent in their self-pity. In fact, the sons decided to accelerate their efforts so as to counter their fathers' rapid decline. As the fathers' skin continued to dry and flake off, and as they lost the last strands of their hair, the sons withdrew deeper into their gloom and doubled their beer drinking. The sons even began to smoke cigarettes again, which they hadn't done in fifteen years, and went so far as to smoke them in the house, despite their fathers' disapproving glares and theatrical coughing jags. Deal with *that.*

As for the fathers, they had retreated so far into their martyrdom that they had become completely detached from their sons and themselves. They did not feel joy when the divorcees swarmed around them at the basketball games; they did not feel terror at the sight of their own jutting ribs and skeletal faces in the mirror; they did not feel pity or anger at the sight of their sons wallowing in their own misery. The only thing that mattered to the fathers was their devotion to starving themselves, and the cold, whipping fall wind which made their bones feel like ache itself.

Thus, the standoff continued—the fathers losing weight at an incredible rate, the sons drinking Herculean amounts of beer and chain-smoking carton after carton of cost-cutter menthol cigarettes— until mid-December, when the people from social services came to inquire about the fathers' condition. Sitting around the fathers' kitchen tables, the social workers explained that the fathers had attracted a great deal of attention, walking around town, looking like displaced famine victims, taking very tiny steps on their way to Raiello's newsstand so as not to slip on the icy sidewalks and break their obviously brittle bones. The social workers then paused, so as to give the sons the opportunity to explain their fathers' obvious physical deterioration.

"Uh-huh," the sons said.

"Come on," each social worker said. "I can see your father." The social workers then pointed at the fathers, who were leaning in the doorways, their cheeks completely caved in, their eyes hanging low in their sockets like Carolina moons, their lined flannel shirts hanging like drapes from their bony arms and sunken chests.

"Uh-huh."

"Fine," each of the social workers said. "Here's our theory: You've stopped feeding your father. You're starving your father to death. You're killing your father and now we know it and you're going to go to jail."

At this point, the sons began to realize the gravity of their situation, and dissembled expertly. The fathers had retired from their own jobs at the fiberglass plant and paper mill several months before, the sons explained, and since they'd retired, the fathers had been acting very strange: beginning projects around the house and then abandoning them, listening to books on tape, writing outraged letters to the editors of national news magazines, starving themselves.

"Starving themselves," the social workers repeated flatly.

"Exactly," each of the sons said. "I figure it's all just part of the normal adjustment period. I figure he'll get over it soon. You know, he'll eat when he gets hungry. That kind of thing."

"You leave us no choice," the social workers said. "We're calling the police."

"*O.K.,*" the sons said, because this was a familiar impasse and they knew exactly what they had to do. Each of the sons, since adolescence, had periodically been caught in these kinds of compromised positions and had tried to wiggle their way out of it and failed badly and therefore had no choice but come totally clean and just tell the truth. And so they told the truth. They explained how badly they had behaved, how miserable they had made their fathers, and how their fathers had decided to starve themselves because of it.

"It's our fault," the sons admitted. "Satisfied?"

"God," the social workers said, looking in bewilderment from the sons to the fathers and back to the sons again. "Is all that really true?" they asked the fathers.

"Yes," the fathers said. Upon hearing their sons' confessions, the fathers felt the fog of their detachment lifting and they also felt a pride in their sons that they had not felt in a long time. Despite their horribly weakened conditions, the fathers walked over to where their sons were sitting and put their hands on their boys' shoulders in a show of support.

The social workers were absolutely baffled by this turn of events, and were forced to consult their social services manuals. Sons starving their fathers, they knew about; fathers starving their sons, they also knew about. But they had no experience with fathers starving themselves because of their sons.

After finding no reference of such a crime in their manuals, the social workers decided to wash their hands of the whole business.

"You're on your own," they said, and fled the fathers' houses so as not to witness anything else that fell outside the boundaries of their manuals.

After the social workers departed, the sons, as in a fairy tale, fell into a deep, deep sleep. When they woke the next morning, they discovered that they had slipped into something like amnesia: once they had admitted to their own irresponsibility, it seemed, the sons had forgotten why it was they were so dissatisfied in the first place. The sons jumped up off their couches and looked around their fathers' houses in complete confusion. "How did I get here?" they said. "It feels like I have been away somewhere."

Then, after the sons oriented themselves and remembered some of the details of their disgruntlement, they looked out the front window. The sun was glinting through the iced-over windows and the light in the room was spectral. "What is my problem?" each of the sons said. "God*damn* it's nice out. What am I doing in here?"

With that, the sons went into a frenzy of self-improvement. They shaved and showered and shoveled their fathers' driveways and shoveled their neighbors' driveways. When they were done, the sons went down to the paper mill and the fiberglass plant and asked for their old jobs back. When asking didn't work, the sons *begged* for their jobs back. After a sufficient amount of groveling and after they had willingly surrendered large chunks of dignity and unused vacation time, the sons were given back their jobs. The sons acted very pleased indeed, and privately pledged to work hard and ignore the harsh job conditions that made them hate the jobs in the first place.

The fathers were, of course, tickled with their sons' transformation, and the fathers were also pleased that their extreme behavior had helped bring about this change. But still, they did not put a stop to their starvation. It just seemed like so much *work* to start eating again, and the fathers were just so damn *tired*. As their sons sacrificed themselves to the idea of their own self-improvement, the fathers looked on and asked themselves: "Can I do that? Am I too old to start over?"

These were serious questions, and so the fathers held another emergency meeting. Attendance was poor, however, and besides, the fathers had gotten so used to their starvation that they could not fathom life without it. It was decided, after a desultory show of hands, that Yes, the fathers were too old to start over, and that they should continue to starve themselves. It was also pointed out, however, that the sons were trying mightily to right the listing ships of their adulthood, and it would be wrong to distract the sons with the terrible details of their fathers' final withering days.

"Let's just keep it to ourselves," the fathers said. And they did. The fathers acted as optimistically and energetically as possible, and didn't moan at all while climbing the stairs or getting out of bed. And when they had to spit blood into their yellowed handkerchiefs, the fathers did so very discreetly, and then washed the handkerchiefs *immediately*. Unfortunately, as December wore on and as the cold tore at the fathers' throats and their listless hearts began to beat slowly, very slowly, the fathers found that they could no longer hide the severity of their starvation. So the fathers simply retreated to their bedrooms, where they wouldn't bother their sons, and where they could die without making a scene of any kind.

As for the sons, they had begun to feel somewhat dead themselves. Their jobs—with the grinding routine and low wages and disregard of health codes and abundance of chemical waste—were as dispiriting as ever. Worse, when the sons tried one last time to reconcile with their wives and children, the wives summoned the reserves of their newly filled reservoirs of self-worth and laughed at their estranged husbands. "The kids don't want to talk to you and I'm glad," the wives said. "You'll be getting the divorce papers soon. Have a good life."

"What's the *point?*" the sons asked themselves after being rejected by their wives. Feeling themselves at the very lip of desperation, the sons nearly slipped back into misery and self-pity. But no, the sons decided, they were through with that. "Besides," they told each other on the telephone, "look at our fathers. Just look at what horrible shape they're in." The sons laid down their phones, went upstairs, and looked at their fathers lying in bed. The fathers each weighed less than one hundred pounds at this point, and were completely swallowed up by their green wool Army blankets; but still, the fathers waved heroically from their beds and insisted they were feeling fine, just fine. "Don't worry about me one bit," each father gasped.

The sons closed the doors to their fathers' bedrooms, went downstairs, and picked up their phones. It was true, the sons admitted to each other, their fathers were in absolutely awful shape. "But that's not the point," the sons told each other. "The point is that they aren't complaining. Where do we get off complaining if they aren't? They've had it worse than any of us." Thus, the sons rallied around their fathers' stoicism, shamed themselves out of their self-pity, and pledged to keep on keepin' on.

. In this fashion, the fathers and sons endured until the day the fathers finally died, the day before Christmas, when an ice storm blew down off the Adirondacks. It was the kind of really severe ice storm that pulls down all your power lines and plays hell with your favorite swamp willow and sends school buses skidding into swollen rivers. The fathers woke up early that morning. They looked outside, saw the ice covering everything and remembered similar storms and felt a last, fierce burst of youthful optimism. The fathers put on their coats, hats, and gloves; they grabbed pickaxes out of their cellars and went outside to hack away at the two inches of ice coating the driveway. But, of course, the axes weighed nearly as much as the fathers. When the fathers tried to lift their axes and have at the ice, they lost their balance and fell. Hard. Their bones cracked and splintered, puncturing their paper-thin skin, and their hearts and lungs lurched, died, and then lurched again, and their whole, treacherous bodies went catatonic with the cold and the pain.

That's how the sons found them, an hour later, lying on the driveway. The sons knelt down on the ice next to their fathers. What now? the sons asked themselves. Should I move him? I probably shouldn't move him. What should I do? The sons, who believed their fathers invincible and never thought they would actually *die*, felt themselves slipping into another, alien world of hurt at the notion that they would soon have to live on this earth without their fathers, and the fathers felt the hurt, too, and wanted to say: "Please don't let me die. I didn't want to starve myself. But I just couldn't stand it, seeing you so miserable and childish. I raised you once; I couldn't do it again. And then you got better, and I was still miserable. I couldn't stand that, either. But that doesn't mean I want to die." And the sons wanted to say: "I'm all fucking alone, and it's the day before Christmas. Are you really going to leave me alone like this?"

But it was too late to say any of this stuff, and the fathers and sons knew it. After all, they had been following the script of father-son relationships for so long that they had grown to like the script, to *trust* it, and they certainly couldn't abandon the script *now*. So the fathers did the only thing they could: they lay there stoically. And the sons did the only thing *they* could: they leaned down and gathered up the pieces of their fathers—the splintered bones, the rattling lungs, the terrible failing hearts—and held them until they died.

She Loved
to Cook
but Not Like This

You might know me: I am the man who burned down the Emily
Dickinson House in Amherst, Massachusetts, and who in the process killed two people, for which I spent two-plus years in prison and,
as letters from scholars of American literature tell me, for which I will
continue to pay a high price long into the not-so-sweet hereafter. Then
again, you might not know me at all: it is difficult to achieve notoriety
in Massachusetts, with all its Kennedys and its tragic sports teams. And
except for that one moment, I am not so special. My father, as you'll
see, was never much to me, and is not special either. But my mother is
worth knowing. She could tell a story, and the story she told was about
the Emily Dickinson House, which is why I'm telling you all this now.

My mother always talked about Emily Dickinson's house in terms of
last gasps, of children vanished and sadly forgotten, of the last drop, drop,
drop of big and small, new and used bodies down a lonely and
unforgiving chasm. When I was a child and then older, she told me
increasingly long and horrific stories about unlucky, stupidly curious
children; trespassing, beer drinking, vandalism-on-the-brain teenagers;

strangers, out-of-towners who didn't know how dangerous the house could be, who paid for their ignorance with an expected, if not exactly warranted disappearance. When I was nine, the stories were more scare than gore, the disappearances clean, neat, complete; the victims' howls unheard over the creaking of that venerable hell-house. When I was nine, my mother concerned herself mostly with the outsiders: men with shady pasts, faded jeans, outstanding warrants, and Marlboro whispers. They were distanced from me and maybe from her as well: arriving as hitchhikers or bus riders, looking for a place to sleep, a place to work, not voting, not paying taxes: unknowable and unknowing. For them, the Emily Dickinson House didn't loom or threaten, but only existed for their temporary use: another big old house with easy locks, daytime occupancy, and a dust problem. Their forced entries were casual, experienced; their disappearances were not that surprising. They were dull victims to me, like casualties of war, monsoons, and other alien disasters. I didn't know them or anyone like them, and their loss affected me only as long as the story lasted. Once they and their threat were sucked into the house and the story ended, then so did my concern for them. These were stories, big and detached, easy on a child's nightmare mind.

You should know here that these men of my mother's stories were not at all like my father, which was the point. My father was not a convict, did not smoke, and never wore blue jeans. My father was an editor for the medium-sized university press in town. He mostly edited books on musicology. He wore khaki pants and was prematurely bald. In addition to his books, my father also covered the area's annual squeeze-box festival for the local newspaper.

"Brady," he once asked me. "Do you know why the accordion is so important? Do you?"

I was seven at this point. I didn't know anything about anything and told my father as much.

"Because it is part of the history of music and immigration," he said. "The Acadians played it, and when they moved from Canada to Louisiana, they brought their squeeze-boxes with them. The accordion is their instrument. It is their gift to the world."

"It hurts my ears," I told him.

I found out later, much later, from my mother, that this comment pretty much unraveled my father. He could not live knowing that his son did not admire his occupation. I was seven, let me remind you. But regardless, my father left the editing and musicology business and searched around for something else to do, something I might respect him for. Somehow, he decided that I would respect him if he became a farmer. Amherst, Massachusetts, is not exactly the country. But my father turned our three-quarter-acre backyard plot into a mini-breadbasket anyway. For six months—May to October—my father grew beets, zucchini, tomatoes, pumpkins, garlic. Our backyard was teeming. But we never ate any of it. My mother still bought our food at the Stop & Shop. The thing is, my father wouldn't let us eat any of the vegetables he had grown. He said we couldn't quote reap the harvest unquote until the time was right.

"When will the time be right?" I wanted to know.

When I asked this, my father looked at me in complete surprise, as if he were hoping all along that I would tell him when he should pick his vegetables. I was eight at this point, but even I could tell that my father didn't know what he was doing; or maybe he didn't want to harvest his crops because he was afraid that the vegetables would some-how be *wrong*. Anyway, that night my father told my mother that he needed to go out in the world and find something worth doing, something that would make us—she and me—proud of him.

My mother told my father that if he sliced himself open, stuffed himself with his accordions, concertinas, and his rotting vegetables, and then hung himself on a pole in the middle of his miserable little garden, then he would probably make one impotent, homely-looking scarecrow.

My father left the next day. I haven't heard from him since. Right after he left, my mother started telling me stories about the Emily Dickinson House and the exotic convicts it swallowed whole. I'm here to tell you that if these stories were supposed to make up for my father's absence, then they did what they were supposed to.

When I was eleven, the escaped criminals of the world left my mother's stories and the children arrived: always a boy and a girl, always nice enough, never too much older or younger than I was. They held hands and raced on foot and yelled sarcastic, innuendo-ridden taunts at each other, things they'd heard and seen at the movies, on television, from their friends who'd heard them in the same places and who changed them and made them their own.

These boys and girls went over to each other's houses after school, on weekends and national holidays. They gave each other cards on birthdays and talked on the phone for hours in alternately soft and dramatically loud voices. And one day when they walked past the Emily Dickinson House, the back door was open, which was unusual, and so they decided to check it out. As they crossed the threshold, as my mother told it, the door slammed behind them, and the big house hummed like the warming up of an oversized garbage disposal. There were screams this time, faint but distinct, and when my mother finished the story I would let out a long sour breath and whine "But it's so unfair." And my mother would nod and say, *"Emily Dickinson's House is like the last hole of a miniature golf course. Like the ball on that final hole, the children go in and then the game waits for someone else."*

My mother and I did a lot of miniature golfing together at this time—on weekends, when I had done well in school, when one or both of us were lonely—and these last lines proved that these children, like me, were young and without stain and played games with great seriousness. That they were me. The story had grown in-line with my own maturation. It told me that strangers were for younger children, that big boys deserved and could handle stories with a moral and other violent personal applications.

When I was fourteen and a half, my mother found herself a boy-friend. His name was Paul, and he taught Cultural Studies at Amherst College. Like my mother, Paul was divorced. He also wore jeans and smoked cigarettes and seemed in every way unlike my father as I remembered him. Paul and my mother were happy for a while. They said their love was just like it was supposed to be the first time. They said this same thing over and over again.

When I was fourteen and a half, my mother and Paul liked to come home after long nights of drinking whiskey at local biker bars or sweet, foreign coffee at college cafés and sit quietly on the couch, waiting for me to finish playing my computer games. I was absolutely gone over computer games—Pong, Asteroids, and the like. I would sit on the floor so I could be close to the screen, furiously working the game's joystick. I was convinced that if I didn't push that joystick to the point of breaking that it wouldn't work right—that it would respond to its own wants, play its own game.

I was rarely a winner at these games, and when the screen flashed GAME OVER I started again. I wanted to reach a point where I won the galaxy more than I lost it.

Paul and my mother nightly would sit behind me patiently, waiting until I made a mistake serious enough to end the game. When I did, I would put the joystick down, turn off the television, and swivel around to face them. They would talk about their evening together, about where they walked, who and what they saw, how beautiful and warm and clear the night was, and how comfortable things were. Paul, because he knew about my and my mother's history of storytelling and because he thought he liked me, would look at me and say: "Hey, have you heard this one?" like he was telling a joke. Then my mother would come to his and my rescue, working in the story like it was part of the patchwork of the evening, like they walked to the Black Sheep Café past the Emily Dickinson House and it reminded her of the time that two kids from the high school (again a boy and a girl—"mere babes" my mother called them) bought a six-pack of Knickerbocker beer and decided to test the waters.

These were the young children grown up, still nice but not quite as nice as they might have been. My mother always stressed that these kids thought too much about what they were doing and what they'd like to do. Their fall lay in the calculation. They walked and made out at the same time, hands inexperienced but confident on each other's waists. The boy carried the six-pack in a plastic bag with handles, and had a mini-crowbar in his jacket pocket. He was secure in his physical self-confidence and his equipment so that if he couldn't blow the door down, he'd pry the lock. The door usually gave way easily, although sometimes it would not cave in when the boy kicked at it, and the crowbar was put to good use.

When I was fourteen and a half, my mother's stories both hardened and became easier, less tense but more gruesome. Bits of bone, flesh, tendon began flecking the walls, crawling under dressers, hopping into the mail slot and sticking there: a cruel change-of-address notification. Imitation gold rings, baseball hats, hair bands, condoms, and full beers were found conspicuously in open view, leftovers, the breathing out after a long swallow. A reminder of the evil of trespassing and its punishment. The story's silences became more meaningful in that they led to excruciating cries, piercing for one second and then brutally cut short. When my mother was too spent to continue, the story ended to a mixed reception of relief and wonder—both hers, I think, and mine. There was never any obvious moral in those stories about vandalism, drinking, or teenage sex—no subliminal abstinence message, no "not here, not now"—and I don't believe my mother intended there to be. But I found one anyway, and I told myself that if I were to ever have sex, which seemed unlikely, that it would never happen in the Emily Dickinson House.

One night, after one of these stories, I heard Paul talking to my mother in the living room. As I said earlier, Paul was a professor at the college. That night he talked to my mother about her odd fascination with brutality, her implicit affirmation of the role of violence in American folklore, her fictional dismemberment of young wayward women as part of the puritanical impulses of late capitalism. He was stern and earnest, and when he talked it was as if he said "Shame." There was a pause before my mother told him that they were just stories and that I was old enough and ready for them. That I would know they were just stories. She sounded surprised, as if Paul had told her that her clothes were on backwards, and that he had been mean about it. The pause before she answered him was as if my mother had inspected herself and found her clothes the way she had always worn them.

That night my mother told Paul that he should go home, that she would call him the next day or maybe the day after, which she never did. But she kept on telling me the stories, and I was glad.

When everything happened, when I did what I did to the Emily Dickinson House, and the judge did what he did to the last two-odd years of my life, and what was done was done, I tried to blame my mother for starting me off on these stories too young. All I wanted was to be and see those sorry lost children, and so instead of telling me stories she should have encouraged me to make friends and play ball, or something. My mother should have made sure that I was normal. So for more than two years I sat in my cell and blamed the cell itself on my mother's active imagination.

But I was normal and I had friends and we all played ball together and, like playing ball and having friends, the stories were part of my childhood, just as stories like the ones my mother told me are part of most people's childhood. I now realize that it wasn't her fault and it wasn't really mine either.

By the time that I was eighteen, I was bored and curious about all the things I didn't know firsthand, and that was all.

In November of the fall of my senior year in high school, I entered the Emily Dickinson House for the first of two times. It was Veterans Day and I had the day off from school. I was eighteen, a year rumored to have something to do with independence. So I walked down Main Street and paid my two-dollar entrance fee like everyone else. It was that easy. It was that boring, to tell the truth. And because it was so boring, I became convinced that it was not the house that was at fault, but my way of entering it. That I was doing it wrong.

When I was eighteen, there were two women of unguessable middle-age who gave tours—the type of people who coughed into the back of their hands and started off their sentences with the phrase, "In this day and age." They greeted me at the door immediately, as if they were afraid I'd break something if left alone. They touched my arm, soft but firm, and asked me to sign their guest book ("Her" guest book), and I did what they asked. I signed *Sidney,* from *Baton Rouge,* which I thought sounded mysterious and a little menacing. One of the women looked at my writing and said, "Nice to meet you, Sidney," and I didn't speak for the rest of the tour for fear of not sounding Southern.

In the entryway of the Emily Dickinson House there was a portrait on the right wall of an old man in a blue uniform, caged in by a wood frame which was stained to look more expensive than it was. His face was hard-boiled from canvas wrinkling and artistic contrivance. A sword lay crossed over his breast, its tip almost touching his right cheek. His eyes were full of the fear of God and not much else. This soldier looked like if he knew you he'd hate you, and he was the most interesting tangible part of the house if my two dollars are worth anything. The two ladies didn't mention him on the tour, keeping him to themselves and to the house. I got the feeling that when they were alone, the tour guides talked to that old war hero in hushed tones and he ignored them, and that this had been going on for years. That it was a longstanding flirtation, a one-sided romance of the least dangerous kind.

The rest of the house, during waking hours, was all information. They talked about the place and its former occupant in small, ineffectual doses.

She played the piano here.

You can picture the garden. She loved to grow things.

Her father replaced this bedroom door when Emily was twenty. She had complained of a draft.

Emily cut her own hair. This is what those scissors would have looked like.

The only other people on that first tour were a group of students and their teacher from someplace named Dickinson College, and they signed their name Dickinson in the guest book and laughed. One of the tour guides greeted them by saying, yelling practically: "You must be the group from Dickinson, but not our Dickinson." To which a student replied, "Ah, but there is only one, isn't there." It went on like that. The teacher had a pack of cigarettes in her shirt pocket and tossed a lighter from one hand to the other as she walked. The students all wore ski jackets.

Maybe I should explain something. Unlike these young scholars, I was not so interested in Emily Dickinson's poetry. I mean, I had read it in high school, but I was not impressed. All those hyphens and capital letters and flies buzzing and death personified did nothing for me. Nor was I so crazy about the figure of the insane, closeted genius so popular on T-shirts and in the minds of young antisocial romantics. Maybe if I were more like these kinds of people, I would not have been so damn bored as we walked from room to room in loose single file. There was a parlor of old books and chintz chairs to the left of the entryway, then a nice set of stained oak stairs that climbed to the second floor, which contained things all second floors do: there were four bedrooms, a study, and a bathroom. The students were hot for Emily Dickinson's bedroom in particular. They felt the flannel white top sheet, stretched taut on an ordinary bed; they cooed at the white dress hung formally on an ornate hanger on the closet door; they nodded at the sturdy oak desk sitting in the corner, covered by an old red spreadcloth which was dotted with fading white daisies; they looked at the built-in bookshelf and its ratty old books and someone tossed off a quote or some poetic turn of phrase, and then there was absolute quiet.

The tour guides told stories. There was one about Emily Dickinson being too shy to endure an examination by the family physician, so she had him stand in the room while she ran past the doorway, naked. I had heard that one before and didn't believe it and didn't think I was supposed to. Belief wasn't the point. There was one about a scholar, a man with an initial for a first name and an initial for a middle name, who visited and "positively swooned" while he was in the bedroom. The guides said that if Emily had married, it would have been to someone like him. This story wasn't a matter of not believing, but not caring. Then there was a story, not really a story but a series of loosely connected images, that I actually remember because it was on a pamphlet, free with paid admission. Over the years I have memorized it, verbatim, for its absurdity, for its part in my own story. The part I know best goes: "But when the poetic impulse struck her, as it so frequently did, we can imagine her snatching up the first used envelope she could lay her hand on (in those years paper was somewhat scarce) or a wrapper of Swiss chocolate with a precious unprinted side, and writing down the fresh new lines while the gingerbread baked but was not allowed to burn." I like this because it is awkward and arcane and because it tells you these inadequate things as a way of introduction, as a way of getting to know someone who is dead, already and forever. But I also like the story because it reminds me of when my mother would burn the hell out of our dinner, which she often did, smoke alarm blazing, smoke, grit, and burnt food pushing into our eyes, into our ears, under our fingernails. When this happened, my mother would cough, laugh, and sing out: *She loved to cook but not like this.* She would then repeat this line softly and more or less to herself, as if it were something she had heard on the radio and was trying to figure out if her lyrics were the right ones—and if not, if she liked her words better. For my mother, the phrase reminded her of something before me, something I wasn't privy to—and because I didn't know its origins, to me it was about her. So when I heard the story of Emily Dickinson cooking gingerbread, it made me think of my mother, of her bad cooking and her mysterious lyric, and it always will.

Of course, Emily Dickinson not-burning the gingerbread also reminds me that I burned down her whole house, which means this story is a little nearer to where it's headed. As that tour wound down I lagged behind and looked for holes, cracks, fissures. I searched for locked doors, loose planks, revolving bookcases. I looked front-to-back, side-to-side. I stopped to examine a picture that hung crookedly. There was a wire attached at two points in the back of the picture, and a nail in the wall that the picture hung on. But there was no wall safe or hidden message behind the picture. There was nothing at all mysterious or sinister. I walked down the stairs with a regret of two dollars spent and lost. Both of the tour guides shook our hands, urged us to sign up for the Emily Dickinson House mailing list; they made us promise we'd come again. Soon. I let the Dickinson group walk out noisily in front of me, and before leaving I looked back and watched the tour guides open a door and enter a part of the house that they had not mentioned during the tour. There was a large set of keys hanging on a hook near the picture of the old war horse, and I took them as I left, closing the door softly behind me.

· · ·

When I returned that night to the Emily Dickinson House, it was dark outside except for the moon, and there were no lights on inside the house. I was by myself. I had thought about bringing someone along— one or several of my friends, a girl named China whom I knew and wanted badly, in the way boys are supposed to want girls with exotic names and their own cars, which China also had. But if I asked any of them, it would have been in the normal terms of vandalism, drinking, lying on flannel sheets, laughing loudly and whispering in the dark and so on. None of which I was interested in. I wanted to look around, to see what the house held for me, to follow my curiosity unexplained and without justification. I knew that if I weren't by myself someone would eventually ask why I had stolen the keys, what I was looking for, and I would have to answer *I just thought of it* and *I'm not sure* and those answers would only bring more questions. They would think I was being strange, and they would be right because curiosity is a strange and normal thing. The more you explain it the more devious it begins to sound. I began trying keys in the lock, doing my best not to look around and act nervous, until the fourth key finally caught and turned.

There were large first-floor windows facing the street in the Emily Dickinson House, and on certain nights they caught the moonlight and held it. It was one of those nights. I could see perfectly without turning on the house lights, without even having to use the flashlight I had brought with me. I decided to check out the upstairs first, postponing a look at the downstairs room, and as I walked the floorboards creaked and coughed, but not any louder than you would expect. The wind was strong and loud for November anyway, softening my footsteps, filling the house with normal, old house noises.

When I reached the top of the stairs, I walked through each bedroom and the study. I ran my hands along the spines of the books, looked at myself in the bathroom mirror. And although it wasn't much more exciting than in the daytime, the night eased the hospital-type jaundice, the specter-yellow that blanketed everything during the day. I began to take back what I had thought on the tour, glad to have seen the place alone. I was also relieved by the idea that simple, honest curiosity could go unpunished. I walked down the stairs, questioned whether I wanted even to look behind the double doors on the first floor. Then I thought that I probably would never be back, and that I should see everything there was to see.

I pushed the doors open and saw that the room was divided into offices: there was a hallway and two offices on either side of it, hidden by shut doors. I casually opened the first door on my left, and as it opened there was a sick, dim light and what seemed to me then an awful scream. As I stood there confused, more or less in the middle of the room, a figure rose up from behind what looked like a desk. The figure was hazy through that dim light. It lurched toward me and in a timeless, overplayed panic I swung my flashlight—a heavy, long-handled Black & Decker—and I connected, and the figure fell. There was another scream. The light, as if voice-activated, vanished almost completely and then grew bigger, and through it another figure showed itself. I swung my flashlight again and hit that figure, too. Then, I ran. I ran out of the house and into the back parking lot, out onto the street, past some people parking their car, back to my house. I stayed there, telling myself I believed none of it, dismissing the violent spectacle of the things I'd seen and done. Then I heard the fire trucks. I followed their noise, as glassy-eyed and emotionless as your best textbook zombie, back to the Emily Dickinson House and watched it burn to the ground, despite the best work of the Hamden County Fire Department. And then I watched as they dragged what turned out to be the remains of one of the tour guides and her lover: fresh from sex on the floor by candlelight; fresh from being knocked unconscious by a blow to the head; fresh from being burned to death. When the candles had fallen, they lit the drapes on fire, and then everything wood in the house, which was pretty much everything, and then everything human, too. The tour guide and her man ended up being not much more than bone and some connective tissue.

I associate sex with the secrecy and punishment of my mother's stories. I also associate sex with the smell of burning flesh. I have never had sex. There is a real possibility that I never will.

As the house burned, I put my head in my hands and cried softly. But because there was a big crowd and other people doing the same thing, it took some time and some truly guttural sobbing before a police officer finally noticed me. He asked me if I was all right and that's when I turned myself in. I said *It's me you want.* It turned out, of course, that they did. I went to the holding pen first, then out on bail, and then back in court. The charge was manslaughter, and the trial was short. I admitted everything, believing most of the bad things the prosecution said about me: confirming through my silence that I was indeed a trespasser and more, that I was without remorse. When 'Guilty' was read it was like a pill, something I had asked for and was finally given after an overlong wait. Before I went off to the state prison at Holyoke, my mother grabbed my hand and told me "It was an accident," and I said "Yes," knowing that that detail made no difference.

I've been out of jail now for two months. My years in prison were nothing you haven't heard before and so I won't bother telling you that story now. I am back living with my mother. She, of course, blames herself for my crime and punishment and I, of course, tell her she shouldn't. She also is happy to see me, and I her. But we both know that I don't have much of a future, the story of twenty-one-year-old fatherless virgin ex-cons who live with their mothers being pretty much set in stone. So I won't bother telling you that story either. But I will tell you what happened the day I got out of prison. The day I got out, I headed right down to the house of the other tour guide, the one who did not die in the fire.

"I have guests," she said after I knocked on her door and she answered. "What do you want?" The old tour guide stood in the doorway and did not ask me to come inside her big old Victorian house, and I didn't ask to be let in. I just stood there, head bowed, on her front porch.

"I want you to know how badly I've suffered," I told her. "I've come to tell you the story I'll tell when I'm an old man." Then I closed my eyes and told her everything I've just told you.

When I was finished with my awful little tale, I opened my eyes and said: "That's the story I'll tell when I'm an old man."

The tour guide for the Emily Dickinson House was not impressed, knowing as she did at least part of the story already. "That's the story you're telling now," she said. "You're telling it before you're old enough to."

"I'm honing it. I've been honing it in prison for over two years now, and by the time I am an old man, it will be perfect."

"How old are you now?"

"I'm twenty-one. I turned twenty-one today. It's my birthday."

The old tour guide was visibly agitated at the thought of me coming to her house, knocking on her door, interrupting her tea parties and book club meetings, telling my horrible story on her front porch everyday until kingdom come. And so she said: "I tell you what, son. Since it's your birthday, and since my guests and I were just sitting down for some cake, I'll invite you in if you promise to never tell that story again."

And since I was lonely and scared of repeating myself and sick at the thought of telling, revising, retelling this story of my life, I promised to never tell it again, and this is the last time.

The Fat

Two men out cruising around in a 1981 Town and Country station wagon. One of these men was eighty-five years old and the other was only thirty, and each of them had problems of their own, but they also shared one serious problem: neither man was successful and neither man was ever going to be successful. The older man was the editor for the Herkimer (NY) *Mountain Enquirer,* and the younger man was his reporter. The older man had been the paper's editor for fifty-two years, but neither his position nor the length of his tenure made him venerable or wizened and he knew it; he also knew that in the scheme of things, he as the editor was less important than the head of advertising, who had a head for numbers and was therefore valuable to the publisher and to the larger world of capitalist enterprise. The reporter was less important than either the editor or the head of advertising. He knew it, too. The station wagon was his. Owning the car didn't make the reporter feel any more important or successful. It had been his parents' vehicle until they decided it was embarrassing for them to drive such a crappy old thing. So they gave it to him.

One of the reasons the reporter wasn't ever going to be successful was that he was out driving around at four-thirty in the afternoon and drinking beer with his equally unsuccessful elder instead of doing his job. He realized that this was the case. But it was hot outside. It was also Memorial Day. Memorial Day was a national holiday. The reporter knew that on national holidays you rolled down the windows in your car and drove around with your buddies and drank warm Utica Club and did not work. This was one of the things he learned in his four years of high school and two years at the state college. He wasn't successful in those places either. But still.

The reporter had realized earlier that same day that he was something of a son of a bitch, which was another reason he was out drinking and driving instead of doing his job. Ironically, the idea came to him while he *was* doing his job. The reporter's job, basically, was to read the stories that came in off the AP wire and copy the most interesting ones, word-for-word, for his own paper. The story that made him realize that he was something of a son of a bitch was a sports story. The AP wire told him that an Ohio State University team mule had gone wild before a College World Series game against Arizona. The mule had tossed its ride, and commenced ramming headfirst into a brick bullpen wall. The mule ultimately broke its neck and died and the Ohio State pep squad carried it off on a stretcher, its legs stiff in a salute toward God.

The reporter, who knew for sure that his job reporting the news was meaningless, somehow still managed to find a great deal of meaning in the news itself. The meaning he found here was that he was exactly like that mule, who was a stubborn son of a bitch who ran headfirst into a brick wall until he *died*. Earlier that day, the reporter's wife had discovered that he had left the oven on overnight. The reporter had done this repeatedly over the two years of their marriage, despite her requests that he remember to turn off the oven whenever he was done using it. It was a *gas* oven, as she told him over and over, and that meant when you left the oven on, you left the *gas* on as well. The reporter's wife had woken him up early that morning just to tell him that he had left the *gas* on again, and that he was an awful, mule-headed son of a bitch. Now he knew what she was talking about.

"I sure am a son of a bitch," the reporter said out loud. It made him feel a little better. When you are working a job that you dislike and are no good at, he reasoned, and the only thing that job can tell you is that you are a son of a bitch and it is a fucking *holiday*, then finally there is nothing to hide from anymore, and you can admit out loud to being what you are. You can also stop doing your job and go drink some beer.

Because of all this new self-knowledge, the reporter was feeling pretty good about himself while he was driving around with his editor. He even felt good about the station wagon, with its tinted windows, deafening exhaust system, and tricky low idle. These were the things he normally hated about his car, which only emphasized his depressing lack of success and his weak hold on a life that actually worked. But now, things being what they were, the car seemed more ornery than pathetic. The car had attitude.

"You are one son of a bitch," the reporter said to the car.

"Say again?" the editor asked him.

The reporter told him the story about the mule and the oven and his wife. The story sounded beautiful and true to the reporter. The world was finally making some sense.

"Chief," he said to his editor. "Let's face facts. That mule is just like you and me. That mule is exactly like real life."

"That mule is dead," the editor said. "Plus, a mascot."

"You don't know what you're saying," the reporter said. "Look at yourself. You, Chief, are a son of a bitch, just like me and the mule. Look at the truth. Just look at it."

The editor didn't say anything back. He simply finished the beer he was drinking and opened another one. The two of them had been driving around for twenty minutes. It was the editor's fifth beer.

The younger turned away from the editor and pretended to concentrate on his driving. He no longer felt like a world-wise, cocky son of a bitch. He felt confused. The reporter had lost all that good feeling so quickly, and the editor had made it happen, somehow. But that was the editor all over. The reporter liked his boss because he had such low expectations of his underlings. Plus, unlike other bosses, the editor did not forbid and actually participated in this very kind of drunken absenteeism. That, the reporter thought, was all right. But other than that, he couldn't understand one thing about his editor. He couldn't understand how his editor could drink as much as he did and still be alive at age eighty-five. He couldn't understand how someone could work the same job for fifty-two years and still be sane, more or less. He couldn't understand how a man could live in the same house all his life, which the editor had also done. And most of all, the reporter couldn't figure out whether the editor was an eighty-five-year-old queerbait who lived all by himself in his dead mother's house, or whether he was just a quirky, lonely, old heterosexual bachelor male. Part of the reporter's job was to open the morning mail. Sometimes in the mail he found catalogues, addressed to his editor, advertising videos with titles like *Boy Toys at Boys' Town* and *Big Thick Dicks*. This made the reporter wonder. Then again, the editor also received catalogues which advertised normal heterosexual porn. Some catalogues advertised both. None of it made any sense. But all in all, despite these mixed signals and despite the reporter's moral revulsion, he still chose to drink beer with the editor and value his companionship and put up with all his crap. And inexplicably, whenever the reporter talked bad about his editor behind his back and made jokes about *fudgepacking* and so on, the reporter felt much worse than he had before the joke was made, even if it was hilarious. None of that made any sense either.

"Yes, I am a son of a bitch," he said, trying to tip the world right-side-up again.

"Give it a rest," the editor said back.

The editor was right. All the reporter's good feelings were gone, and it was probably best to just let them go and go back to being his normal sad self. And what his normal sad self usually did in this situation was to stop off at the Kentucky Fried Chicken so he could use their bathroom for free. This was one course of action the reporter knew his editor would agree with. Both men believed that if you were out driving around drinking all day, then the most satisfying kind of inter-mission was to use a restaurant bathroom without paying for anything. Or you ordered your food—a BLT, say, or a piece of cherry pie—and then stuck a roofing nail in it and started waving your arms like a victim of some great outrage, tossing out terms like *oral surgery* and *lawsuit.* The reporter and the editor had discovered that these threats got you free meals and other, less obvious things.

When the two men came out of the KFC a few minutes later, a good bit of the reporter's car was covered in chicken fat. The fat was glinting and rippling in that late afternoon May sunshine.

"Son," the editor said, "I'm glad that's not my car."

The reporter was not shocked by the state of his car. He just *knew* that this was the kind of the thing that happened to men like himself. He had, of course, *known* about the KFC's exhaust fan, which he had parked right under and which spewed chicken fat all over anyone or thing that was stupid enough to let it. Everyone knew about the fan, which had been the subject of a fierce letters-to-the-editor campaign at the very newspaper where both men worked. Now that the fat had fallen, the reporter knew that things were going to change for the worse. He knew, for instance, that the fat might be the beginning of the end of his car, which didn't even run when it was covered with snow. He also knew that the fat-covered-car might be the beginning of the end of his marriage, which like his car could not take much more of his abuse. It was Monday now, and the reporter knew how the next two days might go. On Tuesday morning, his wife would wake up to find the car, still all covered with fat, in their driveway. She would tell him that the car looked like a bigger version of something you might find in the corner of your damp cellar or in the back of your throat, not something you might find in the classy showrooms of Detroit. She would also point out that the car's fate was typical of her husband, who was irresponsible and selfish and who ruined everything he touched. His wife's reaction is part of the predictable old story of human affection and its rise and ruin, and so the reporter knew that by the end of the day, just as he was deciding that his wife was the most beautiful thing in the world, that he could not possibly live without this true love of his life, and that he was finally going to treat her *right,* then she would decide that he was no longer worthy of her female companionship and that their two years together had been a Complete Fucking Nightmare.

On Wednesday, the reporter knew his wife would begin suing him for divorce.

Of course, the reporter knew that the abuse of his marriage and his car was accidental on his part; but he was smart enough to also know that when chicken fat and automobiles and marriage are concerned, there are no true accidents and that when there are no true accidents, a man must act like a man. What a man would do in this situation, the reporter knew, was to charge back into the Kentucky Fried Chicken and demand some kind of compensation for his ruined car and marriage and *life.* He knew this wouldn't do a damn bit of good, but he did it anyway.

Now, it was true that the editor was lucky enough not to have his car covered with chicken fat. But it was also true that he had enough problems of his own, problems which conspired to take the considerable shine off the fat. One of his problems was not that he was gay, or that he was not gay, but that he couldn't be sure one way or the other. This bothered the editor, who thought that after eighty-five years on this planet you should at least know *something* about your true self. But he didn't know. For instance, he was interested in *glory holes,* which were prominently featured in the catalogues he received at the office. But then again, the editor didn't find it a bit incriminating to be intrigued by a phenomenon in which a man—a big-gutted trucker packing a bowie knife in a leather hip-holster, maybe, or an off-duty state policeman with a mustache—goes into a thruway rest-stop bathroom at one in the morning on a Wednesday and sticks his thing into a hole in a stall divider and actually gets it sucked. The editor found this arrangement interesting, but that wasn't definitive proof of anything. After all, it was interesting, was it not? The editor had watched a PBS special on the marriage rituals of the ancient Incas. He was interested in that subject, too, but that didn't necessarily mean he was interested in marrying an Inca or being one.

What all this indecision did mean, however, was that the editor was very tired of life. This fatigue was his own fault. He had been warned. His mother had told him that this was going to happen some forty-five years earlier. At that point, he was forty years old, had worked at the newspaper for twelve years, and had been editor for two of those years. He had lived at home with his mother for all forty years of his life and showed no interest in leaving. Ever. It didn't seem normal to his mother. Her own husband, the editor's father, was a Mohawk Indian, or half of one. Years before he had left both wife and child to work as a fly on a Manhattan high-rise construction crew for fifty cents an hour. That seemed more normal.

"I'm warning you," she said to her son, "you're going to get truly sick of life the way you're living it."

"I love you, Mother," he told her.

"Don't be ridiculous," she said back. She then wondered aloud whether he also loved the terrible failing economy or the polluted Mohawk River or the polluting paper mills or the niggling, small-town Irish politicos or the starving Presbyterian farmers or the fat Catholic priests or the long, fierce, sometimes beautiful winters that made the farmers and priests and everyone turn to religion in the first place. She wondered whether he loved correcting comma splices and split infinitives eight hours a day, whether he believed not in the ideals of truth and justice, but in the urgency of covering monthly grange meetings and honoring in print the sanctity of the DAR and the Masonic Temple. She wondered whether he loved the prospect of living in the same house for the rest of his life. She wondered how he would feel about becoming a functioning alcoholic, and every Saturday night entertaining the one or two friends that were still alive and not too leery of him to drink his cheap bourbon. He would pour the bourbon, she told him, out of bottles with personalized labels that said: *From the Bar of . . .* " Would he love that, too? she wondered.

"Mother," he had said to her, "you are a pip."

She was a pip. She was also right about his life, which now, forty-five years later, he couldn't wait to get rid of. The editor knew that getting rid of it, just dying, was his only option. Changing his life, he knew, was not really an option. Maybe it would have been an option if he had moved away and lived in someone else's mother's house and worked in high-rise construction. Then, maybe, he would have been able to come back to Little Falls and know whether he wanted to stick his dick into a hole and get it sucked and *like* it. Now, his mother was dead and he had become an alcoholic and printed the booze labels, and all he could be glad about was that he had a friend, a sad, self-destructive somewhat likeness of himself who could get his car covered with chicken fat. The editor was genuinely happy that he had such a friend. Having that friend was maybe the most he could hope for.

The editor had more ambitious hopes when he had hired the younger man two years earlier. After a good half-century of denial, the editor admitted to himself that his long-dead mother had been right: he was truly sick of his life. So he began his Final Failure stage. When you enter the Final Failure stage, you drink as much as a human can, encourage damaging rumors about yourself, and destroy everything you've ever been associated with. This the editor did. He drank whatever and whenever he could, had the porn catalogues mailed to his work instead of his home address, and hired the younger man to write at the newspaper. The editor wasn't sure his new reporter had ever even *read* a newspaper. What he was sure about, on sight, was that the younger man was like thousands of other young men in small towns who go about ruining their lives through their own smallness of mind and body. The editor hoped his new reporter would ruin the paper in the process. Obviously, the new reporter's presence didn't go over too well in the newsroom. The other reporters griped about his incompetence. They said the new guy was a disgrace to journalists everywhere. The editor was in his Final Failure, and so he said that they themselves were talentless hacks and if they had any grievances to mail them to him, care of the Great Beyond.

But the problem with being a Final Failure, the editor found out, was that it wasn't so final. He discovered that it is difficult to drink yourself to death on a timetable. The newspaper was already horrible and so it couldn't lose its integrity or loyal audience or anything. Everyone thought he was at least gay-*like*, and so the rerouted porn didn't reveal anything new about its recipient. And the editor actually started to *like* his new reporter. He thought the reporter liked him back. All this liking retarded the progress of his Final Failure.

The friendship began after the editor had argued with the head of advertising about an ad for the high school football coach's fortieth birthday. The ad was to include an old picture of the coach as a high school player, locked in a three-point stance. The header was to read: *Lordy, Lordy, Look Who's Forty.* The head of advertising said over the phone that the football coach's wife wanted the ad *big* and so it was going to be *big*. It was also going to bump an eight-inch article on heavier-than-normal use of road-salt during the previous winter.

The editor got off the phone, cursing. He turned to the reporter, who was across the room enjoying the spectacle of this profane old man, and said bitterly: "Lordy, Lordy, Look Who's Forty."

"I understand," the reporter said. "Someone feels *sick*, they should go to the *doctor.*"

That sounded all right to the editor. He had no idea what it meant, but that was all right, too. What going to the doctor might have meant was the two of them should go have a few drinks at the Happen Inn, which they did. But the important thing to the editor was he had found someone who talked in code. When someone talked in code you did not have to worry about clarity. You did not have to worry about the difference between a true friend and a drinking friend. You did not have to worry about whether one friend was physically attracted to the other (the editor was), and whether the attractive friend would reciprocate the feelings (the reporter would not). When you spoke in code you lived in the middle of ambiguity, and in the middle of ambiguity you did not have to worry about being certain of anything. Outside of ambiguity, certainty was expected. In the middle of ambiguity, certainty was silly.

What also seemed silly to the editor was that he was actually starting to care about the reporter. The editor realized that this feeling was a little unseemly for someone smack in the middle of his Final Failure. He had hired someone for his comic fuck-up potential and for his infectious self-destructive qualities and ended up *liking* him. This irony occasionally angered the editor, and he sometimes treated his friend like the thick-headed piece-of-work the reporter sometimes was. But at the end of the anger, the editor still genuinely cared for his new friend, and there was nothing he could do about it.

The problem with all this caring, the editor found out, was that he wasn't much good at it. As someone in his Final Failure, the editor was of limited use to someone trying to put his life back together, which the reporter was hoping to do. Over the two years of their friendship, the reporter's life had truly fallen apart, and nightly he begrudged his bad luck in life and in love. It pained the editor to hear this sincere, hurt bitching coming out of his young friend. True, the end of the reporter's marriage seemed imminent and was mostly the reporter's fault. But the editor knew that the marriage was his friend's last tenuous connection to normal life, to a life that functioned the way it was supposed to. The editor also knew that the reporter still loved his wife; even if the marriage itself was beyond the help of love, he felt a responsibility to do what little he could to help his friend.

And so, a week before the fat fell, after a night of bearing witness to some fierce breast-beating over the reporter's impending exile from love, the editor put his hand on the reporter's shoulder, and said: "*I* love you, my friend."

"I know you do, Chief."

And there it was. The editor knew that once you have told your friend you love him and it is accepted, even if both the love and its acceptance are ambiguous, then the least you should do is wait and be willing to comfort the friend after his car has been covered with chicken fat. You should also be sympathetic after the friend has failed to convince anyone that he and his car are worthy of true compensation.

So the editor drank beer and waited for his friend to come out of the Kentucky Fried Chicken.

After a long while, the reporter came out of the restaurant. He looked sadly at his car, which was of course still covered with chicken fat. It was fairly baptized in the stuff.

"I'm apparently owed nothing, not even a free car wash," he said. "That's what she said."

"She said who?"

"The manager. Lydia K."

"Lydia K. sounds like a tough nut."

"True enough. She said I paid for nothing and had nothing coming to me."

"Many are the ways we wound each other," the editor said, patting his young friend on the back. The reporter appreciated the gesture.

"Why not have another beer," he said.

"My friend," the editor said, "that is a super idea."

The station wagon, despite its many faults, was at least big. It was too much of a car to be completely covered by one exhaust fan and its back end was mostly clear of the fat. The reporter opened its rear door and pushed aside all the tire irons, jacks, golf clubs, beer bottles, and general garbage that had been tossed in the way-back. Then he and his boss sat with their feet dangling like boys selling buckets of used golf balls or glasses of lemonade, not like full-blown adult males in the middle of major personal crises. They drank beer for a good while and watched the people leave the Kentucky Fried Chicken with their chicken and change and their mysterious homelives. All this coming and going didn't ease the reporter's sense of crisis much. He noticed all the dirty looks he and his boss were getting from the other folks in the parking lot. He felt like they deserved the dirty looks. They were two grown men who were already drunk, sitting in the back of a station wagon and drinking more beer toward the butt end of a national holiday. They were definitely dirty. The car itself looked like it had just popped out of the uterus of a bigger, mother car. If afterbirth was dirty, which the reporter thought it was, then so was the car. At the moment, he could not imagine anything of his being not-dirty. But the people could get their chicken, level their dirty looks, and then leave and get clean. They left the dirt and in leaving rescued themselves from dirtiness.

"Hop to," the reporter said, standing up. "Let's go somewhere."

"Hold your horses," the editor said, opening another beer.

The reporter sat down sadly. Except for one other car—a light blue Chevy Nova—the parking lot had emptied by this point. He wished *he* could leave the parking lot; but the reporter realized he was not going anywhere without the editor, who was of course in his Final Failure stage and was not going anywhere either. The reporter also realized that he himself was entering the phase of Slow Steady Regret. Being dirty accounted for most of the regret, but unlike being a son of a bitch, knowing *this* truth didn't make him feel any better. He knew that if you were a dirty young man who dropped out of state college and into a small, dying mill town and took on a crappy job and stumbled your way out of love and into a drinking problem, then you did not get out of the phase of Slow Steady Regret so easily. You could try, of course. Six months earlier, his wife had expressed some deep concern about their marriage. She had used the phrases "put up or shut up" and "do or die." And so the reporter had come home early from work. He did not drink, which is what he normally did when he came home from work. Instead, he cooked dinner. Chicken Kiev, toothpicks and all. But then the phone rang, which was upstairs in their bedroom, and the chicken was left alone for much too long and burned. When he came downstairs, his wife was waving a dish towel trying to clear the smoke. She did not look mad. She did not look surprised, either. She looked like she expected him to do something stupid and he did the expected. His wife looked like she expected to come home and find the dirty life she had left and she *found* it.

"Chief," he told his boss. "Life is *dirty*. I need a car wash. I mean it."

"I know you do," the editor said. "Relax. I'll take care of it."

He finished the beer and walked toward the Kentucky Fried Chicken. The editor felt like his own life, despite the porn and the alcoholism, wasn't dirty enough. He wanted *more* dirt and he wanted to be sure about the wanting. But still, the editor knew what the reporter meant. The reporter meant that life had to change. The problem was that the grand or terrific or horrific gestures that are usually seen as Life Changing did not change anything. They made life a little dirtier or not dirty enough. That was all. Change required something else. The first time he had seen his reporter's wife was at the paper's annual Christmas party, a month after the reporter had been hired. She had brown or blonde hair, depending on whether the Christmas lights blinked orange or green. She was beautiful in either light. From across the room, he watched as she smiled and put her right hand on her husband's left cheek and left it there. That gesture changed the editor a little, just watching it from across the room. It changed the way he thought about love, which now seemed slightly possible if still unlikely. It changed the way he felt about the reporter, whom he had regarded as a simple fuck-up and whom he now regarded as a more complicated fuck-up who was somehow worthy of the love of a better person. *That* was what change required. Change required a soft right hand on a left cheek. Change required a free car wash.

And so the editor walked up to the restaurant door and tried to open it, but it was locked. By this point it was after six o'clock, on a holiday after all, and the KFC had closed early without him even noticing it. He pulled and then pounded and yelled for the manager, Lydia K., but she didn't answer the door even though a light was still on inside, and there was still that one car besides the reporter's in the parking lot. Finally, the editor gave up on his quest for the free car wash. He turned to walk back to the station wagon. That's when he saw the reporter standing next to the other car with a tire iron in his hand. It was, the editor realized, a tire iron from the back of the reporter's station wagon.

The editor stood in the doorway of the Kentucky Fried Chicken and waited to see what happened next. If his friend began beating on that other car with the tire iron, then that would be expected—what could be more expected from a dirty, drunken youngish man who believes he's been Wronged By Life?—and it would also then be expected that they would keep on being pathetic and unsuccessful and nothing would change. But if the reporter did not destroy the car, if he put the tire iron back in the station wagon and drove off, if the fat were allowed to settle and harden or crack and fall off or just do whatever it is fat can do, then who knew what might happen? Who knew that the car wouldn't run better if a little fat were left on it? Who knew that *life* wouldn't run a little better? Who knew whether the reporter's wife would begin to see her husband as someone who could successfully do the unexpected? Who knew whether she would fall in love with him again, or fall in love with the editor himself, or the editor with the reporter, or the reporter with the editor? Who knew for sure that someone's Final Failure couldn't be reversed, that the tide of Slow Steady Regret couldn't be turned?

The reporter lifted the tire iron above his head as if it were an ax, and then hesitated.

"Hold on," the editor whispered. He began running toward the reporter, breathing hard, and waving his arms frantically. "Just wait one *minute*," he shouted. The reporter turned to look at the editor, and started laughing; it was the first time he'd seen the editor move faster than a walk. The editor ran like an arthritic crab. But the editor didn't care about the laughing. Let the reporter laugh, just as long as he put down the tire iron. Because if the reporter didn't destroy the car, then who knew how their lives might change? If the reporter could be convinced to put down the tire iron, then who knew what might be possible?

The World Dirty,
Like a Heart

I t all starts with Tull, my so-called friend. He is the real deviant in this group of two. For a while, ours was the same worn path. We were both teachers of high school history. We were both married, had been for some time, and constantly complained about our wives but only in the nicest terms, and never when they were within earshot. We were growing old but not gracefully, wearing baseball hats and jeans slung low and desperately faking youth. Like our students, Tull and I advertised our immaturity through the exaggeration of our likes and dislikes. We both were vocal in our love for cable TV. I was overly fond of my Iroc Z, and Tull denounced public transportation as something communist.

Then Tull found a girlfriend. I say "girlfriend" and not "lover," "other woman," or some other this-and-that because she was just seventeen and adulthood was still only a rumor. This was three months ago. He told me and I couldn't believe it. I still don't know what to think. It's a complicated issue. There are the not-so-tender forces of law and morality to consider. Then there is love. All I know for sure is that I don't have a seventeen-year-old girlfriend, don't really want one, and why the hell should I? What makes you so sure that I'm that kind of man, anyway?

Her name was Leslie Surprise. She was a senior, and Tull said she had an eye for detail. Leslie was being courted by the community college. She had cheekbones that build and break nations. Her ankles looked sleek and thoroughbred-powerful in sheer stockings. She was an ace at long math, and her voice was such that it made sarcasm sound like seduction. "Your future," the community college told her, "lies in Travel and Tourism." They promised her a free ride, bonus mileage, and the opportunity to cultivate an informed world view.

I thought Tull was the worst kind of fool, and I told him so. But he was taken. He said he was in-love serious, that he was even thinking about quitting something. Tull's first thought was alcohol, one of his dearest if most worrisome passions. "Lent," he said. "I'll give it up for Lent, and that'll be it."

I reminded him that Lent had already passed and that he would have to wait a year.

"Sooner, then. Memorial Day," he said. He was all of a sudden crazy for abstinence. I could hear the creak of his mind's machine, busy manufacturing other kinds of sacrifice. It was the height of bowling season. He was a fair bowler. Tull would forsake bowling for love.

"What will Judy say?" I asked him. Judy was his wife, a tough county lawyer who believes in Hammurabi and thinks due process an experiment failed.

"Bam!" Tull said. "Fireworks." He didn't seem to mind.

"How?" I wanted to know. "Where?"

"In my room during periods seven and eight. I was explaining the Louisiana Purchase. She wanted to know what we bought and how much it cost. I told her, territory by territory, and each time she said, 'Was it worth it?' Then she kissed me. Once on the cheek, then once where it counts."

"What the hell does that mean?" I was already repulsed. Every August during faculty orientation, the school administrators and psychologists and guidance counselors teach you everything you need to know about little boys and little girls, and it's all bad.

"On the lips," Tull said. "She kissed me on the lips."

"Oh," I said. Then: "What else?"

"Nothing."

"That doesn't sound like love to me," I told him. I'd been expecting much worse.

"You'd be surprised," he said.

Tull and I sat for a while. It was our spring break, noon on a Wednesday, and we were in my kitchen. My wife, Cass, was at work. She is a dental hygienist, works eight hours a day, and I wondered about the secret paths she might follow while we were apart, eight-to-four, Monday through Friday. I wondered what she would think about Tull and Leslie Surprise. I wondered if Cass had her own version of Leslie Surprise: someone younger than me or better looking or more articulate in his desires. I wondered if the world were split between those who acted on their desires and those who did not, and if those who did not were at the absolute mercy of those who did. I wondered just how much I knew about the world. While I was wondering I drank my beer quickly, one, then another. Tull just watched his. It sat on the table and he looked at it as if it were rotating slowly and he was checking its progress. I thought I could see it move myself after a while. It was an extraordinary display, a household miracle so small you couldn't be sure if it were actually happening or what it might mean. I drank that beer, too, and he watched me drink it, smiling. I was thinking. Tull was my friend and I was worried about him in the same way you worry about yourself, except with less attention to detail.

After a few minutes of silence I said, "What about Ronan? Do you remember him? You remember him, don't you?"

Ronan was a business math teacher. He had been a captain of industry, and when he retired, he said he wanted to give something back to the community. That meant he longed to teach business math and they let him, until he was caught in the janitor's closet cozying up with the janitor's collection of low-rent skin magazines. Both Ronan and the janitor were promptly fired, and the school made a big production of buying new mops, buckets, cleaning solutions of all kinds.

"That's different," Tull said. "That was a disgrace. Be serious. Onanism. God's curse. Then there's me and Leslie. Two normal human beings."

"Even worse," I said. "C'mon. You've got to know that history repeats itself. You know that."

"History is a bore," he said.

"You don't know your past, you don't know your future."

"History is flat faced, walleyed, ass-dumb to the world."

I lectured him on wrong and right, on the things and strings of the heart breaking asunder. Then I let him go. Sometimes you have to. Still, I thought about him all break. I feared that Tull, like myself, like all aging men, was a would-be victim of a world that favored youth and beauty and all things new. We were a terrorized lot, oppressed and damned like all the old Jews and Christians, and we were nothing if not vulnerable.

Sure enough, Tull returned from spring break to find himself fired. It turns out everyone knew. They read him the riot act at the school-board meeting. They said his name would be forever linked with perversion. The principal promised to draft a letter to his wife personally. They all asked Tull how it felt to be a pariah, and he told them he hadn't been one long enough to have an intelligent opinion.

"Let me narrate it for you," I said afterward. "Caught. Fired. I'm sure you'll be divorced soon. That's the way it will go. Love."

"You don't understand," he said. "Let me tell you one thing. She loves the way I say Manifest Destiny."

"How do you say it?"

"What?" Tull asked. He appeared to be deep in thought. There was a lot to think about. He had a look of permanent worry.

"I said, how do you say Manifest Destiny?"

"I say it like I mean it."

I went home and told this to my wife. I'd given her daily updates of the whole situation. I am the type of fool who keeps no secrets. I tell

all. The day will come and there will be none of the usual things to hold
against me.

"What the hell does that mean?" Cass wanted to know. "'Like I
mean it?'"

"I have no idea. Can you believe he was so stupid, though? He
honestly didn't believe he would get caught. Either that or he didn't
care."

. "Wouldn't get caught?" Cass said. She couldn't believe that
discovery was all I cared about. She had this furious right-and-wrong
look on her face. Her eyes were menacing slots.

"Poor Judy," I said weakly. I looked straight at my wife. Even at
thirty-four years of age, she has retained an astonishing degree of youth.
At work, Cass wears rubber gloves and a face mask, and she says that
these things help keep her young. They're supposed to protect her from
the elements: from blood and saliva and the prevailing winds of bad
breath. I looked at her and thought of Tull and Leslie Surprise and the
offenses of love and again wondered if I, too, were being used and
abused. The precedent, as in the court of law, had been set. I sat and
looked at her, and the longer I looked the more I loved her and the less
I believed she was true. I began to think of the world as a dirty, clogged
heart, my clean self rejected by it as foreign.

"What is it?" she said. I had been staring at her. "Is there something
on my face? There's something on my face, isn't there?"

"I've got a terrible week coming up," I told her, getting off the
subject. "It's Local History week. I've got to get from Montcalm and the
Battle of Ticonderoga to the Industrial Revolution in two days. Two
days and two hundred years. Did you know that Little Falls produced
more bicycles than any city in the U.S. between 1883–87? Did you know
that Ticonderoga means 'where the lake shuts itself' in Mohawk?"

"Wonderful," Cass said, taking off her stockings. She was rubbing
her toes and paying no attention to me. Cass has beautiful toes, lithe
like fingers. In a world of hammer toes, corns, and sweat rashes, Cass's
toes are something angelic. Even then I wondered who else might be
loving them.

. . .

Anyway, that's Tull and you need to know all of this because of what comes next, the party at Cass's boss' house, which is why I'm telling it. Cass and I went to the party later that same week. Every day after school, I had gone over to visit Tull. He was sitting around, drinking the same beer a sip at a time. His house was dark. It smelled like failure. Tull sat in the dark and said things like, "I'm the worst kind of man. I'm a caught man." He'd even been dropped by Leslie Surprise, who was under psychiatric supervision. Her parents had placed a restraining order on Tull. They would call his house daily and ask, "Is the Devil home?" and then hang up before he could answer.

Tull claimed Leslie was dragging him down. He said she was acquiescing to the forces of popular morality. He called her immature.

"You wouldn't understand," he said. "You've got Cass. You've got love. You've got no problem being normal, and normal has got no beef with you either."

Those were the pressures I faced. I went to Tull's everyday and received the lecher's platitudes and then I went home to Cass every night. The more normal I was, the more beautiful and detached she became.

By the party on Saturday, my heart felt like dead weight, my nerves in active revolt, the rest of my body caught somewhere in between.

It was a dentist party, hosted by Cass's boss and his wife, who was also a dentist. They had a young son, who was in charge of taking and then retrieving the guests' coats at his parents' parties. Both Cass's boss and his wife consider themselves amateur ironists. For instance, Cass's boss likes to say to me, "You know, Harold, there is no dirtier mouth than a dentist's." Then he shakes his head and says, "The world is a cruel place if you want it to be."

I always get plenty drunk when I'm around Cass's boss and his wife. That night, I had three beers before we even left our house, one in the car, a pint of bourbon as a back-up in the glove compartment. I was liquid and morose. I thought of everyone I knew. There was Leslie, Cass, dirty Tull. Who else? My parents. I remembered how they referred to each other only in pronouns. They were dead and beyond judgment, but I mourned all of their failures to be good people. I was bawling right there in the car.

"Don't embarrass me," Cass said. Not that anyone would have noticed one more weepy drunk. Cass's boss always threw knockdown parties and this one was no exception. We walked in, and there was already a fight of the man-and-wife variety going on right in the dining room. It was our hosts and Jesus, what a scene, right in the middle of their annual wingding. Whiz, their voices said. Bang. They were promising terrible things, to rend and tear and to make foolish all words of love, honor, and cherish. Their party guests were present to bear witness, just so no one could say later, after the inevitable divorce, that they never saw it coming.

It was a holy mess. The spider plants were crashed on the dining room floor. Country music—Waylon, Willie, Hank, Sr.—was playing loudly. Everyone complained about it, but no one could find a way to turn it down. In the kitchen, a man I didn't recognize was bent over the sink retching loudly. His wife, or whoever, stood next to him with her hand on his back. She was smoking a cigarette, saying, "That's right. Let it all out. You'll feel much better once it's all out where we can see it." A large crowd had gathered, and no one seemed to believe her.

At some point I lost Cass but found the nitrous tank. I'd heard its sucking noises all night long and was glad I finally found it. The tank was surrounded by dentists holding brightly colored balloons. I got the feeling that they all knew each other from college, dental school, something. They all seemed to have nicknames for each other: Tree-man, Snoopy, Shoe. It occurred to me that they were doing it like they did in college, except not as well and with less joy. This put them all on edge, especially the host. He and his wife had called a momentary truce, and his low-grade shrieks told me that he wanted nothing more to do with time and loss.

"Suck," he said to the man next to him. "Dennis. You're up next. In goes the good air, out goes the bad. Don't be such a sorry old dentist. You're just a tired old fuck, aren't you?"

"Barry," his wife said, coming from behind me, "you're being seven different varieties of asshole."

Round two. More yelling. The man named Dennis dropped his glass. His eyes took on the appearance of two foggy marbles. He offered up his balloon and I took it, inhaled, stopped, and then inhaled once more. I closed my eyes. The room went away for a moment and when it returned it had assumed the texture of a plate broken, and then glued back together.

"Jesus," I said to the man next to me once my head cleared. I had forgotten that dentists had access to such joy.

He agreed. "Oh boy," he said and who knew what he was talking about. I took another hit on the balloon and looked for Cass. The room was filled with smoke and blather. When I finally found her she was in the corner talking to some smooth type wearing a seersucker suit and no shoes. He was gesturing with his beer bottle. It looked like he was lecturing on something of great importance, and he acted like he knew his shit back and front. Cass's face was red. She was rapt. My misery returned. He was good-looking, all right, a handsome young man. I took one last hit and imagined from across the room that this man could speak many languages—Romanian, Polish, Old Low Welsh— and that all of them would bring to Cass's knees a great weakness.

I felt my chances in this life drop to zero.

"Oh God," I said and turned to beg for another balloon. That's when I saw the hosts' son. He was standing off to the side. He was young—ten or eleven, I thought at the time. I found out later that he was in the seventh grade, twelve years old and so what? That's not the point. The point is that he was young and my mind was already full of thoughts and convictions about the boundaries of age and the consequences we face in crossing them.

There was another point. The boy was drinking a beer. Did I mention that? He was drunk and weaving. Once I had assessed the whole situation, I called the father over.

"Your son," I told him, "is drunk."

"He's just tired," he said.

"Just tired? Look at him. He's got a beer right in his hand."

"He's just overtired," Barry said. "It's way past his bedtime." He smiled at his son. Then he walked away.

The boy was red-eyed and considering me from underneath his hair, which was long and had the look of sweat to it. I squatted the way baseball coaches do in front of their young sports. If there had been grass I would have plucked a blade and chewed on it until my gums bled. Here was something I could do. You're a teacher, I thought. Teach. There was beauty to be salvaged in all the ugly places.

"I remember when I was you," I told him. "I remember what it was like. I know what it is to be just yea high to this terrible old world."

"So what?" he said, pointing his beer bottle at my forehead. "You're just one more in a long line of asswipes."

Which is why I slapped him, right across the face. He didn't seem to care, the little monster, stood there like his life had always been that way and that it wasn't half-bad. But his parents sure cared, nitrous oxide and the splintering of their family unit regardless. They raised a stink. Eventually, they made certain everybody knew, school board and parents included. This night, however, they just yelled murder. A crowd gathered. I was on my knees. I looked up, and Cass was there with seersucker. She looked grim, and I pleaded with her in great dramatic fashion. "Where are the waters of childhood?" I asked.

Seersucker answered. He had a foreign accent, Southern maybe. His voice was resonant, like he possessed more than one throat. He said, "Sir, it looks like you've been swimming in them."

And then I hit him too, right in the bread basket of that smart suit, starting another ruckus with me in the middle of it, swearing, "I was wrong, but I'm not sorry. I thought he was a child, but he's no child. He's old and ruined already and I'd hit him again just like I'd beat anyone who's not what they're supposed to be. I tell you, I won't be afraid of this life!"

The school board waited until Tuesday to fire me. Cass left me the next day. She says we're not divorced, but separated. I say I'll do anything for her. I've asked her if she wants to have a baby. I insist that if that's what she wants then I want it too. We'd be great parents, I tell her. I know that this is how marriages are saved every day, but Cass says no. She says she needs some time, is all.

I think we're divorced. I can't help but believe it's true.

Sometimes Cass still comes over on sympathy missions. She finds me on the couch with my pervert friend Tull. His wife Judy has already filed for divorce. Tull and I are starting to believe that the world is closed to us. Whatever hope we have is coming to a slow burn. We stop complaining about it only when Cass is there, just so she'll come back.

When she comes around, Cass tells us stories of the outside. Last week she came over on a Thursday. It was four in the afternoon and there were beers scattered, but she pretended not to notice. I remember how she looked coming in from the bright world. She was in her white uniform and she had the cut and quality of lodestar. I ran over and held her hand and she let me.

"Let me tell you," she said once I had quit my fawning. "There was this guy in today. He was from Colorado. He even showed me his driver's license as proof. He told me while I was working on him that he was a cowboy, retired. I said 'Sure you are,' and he says, 'I'll prove it. I'll tell you something you don't know about us cowboys.' 'Fine,' I said. 'Tell.' Then he says, 'Do you know what we call bull testicles? We call them Rocky Mountain Oysters. Did you know that? They're a delicacy. They're supposed to be an aphrodisiac, too, and I eat them all the time.' That's what he told me. I asked him what they tasted like and he said it was exactly like eating chicken. Have you ever heard of such a thing?"

I was stunned.

"He said that?" I screamed. "Where is this old bastard, talking to my wife that way? I'll kill him, I swear." I glanced over at Tull to share my outrage, but he was staring at Cass. It took me a minute to recognize his look—his eyes glassy, his brow sweaty, his face dumb with want. It was a look full of deep, longstanding, incurable desire—a look I had seen him level at Leslie Surprise—which is why I hit him too, pow, a quick one right in the face, and he grabbed me and pulled me down and while we were wrestling on the floor Cass left. I didn't even see her go.

What We
Won't Do

There are no astronauts born and raised in my town. Maybe if there were, I would not have done the following: destroyed one marriage, two friendships, and my wife's confidence in me as a dependable life-partner. Nor would I have turned an innocent barbecue—the kind of peaceful American backyard outing you'd see in a commercial for Ford trucks or the beef industry—into something you'd see in a professional wrestling steel cage match. But I have done these things, and that's because there are no astronauts born and raised in my town. No olympic figure skaters or beauty queens or I-knew-him-then and look-at-him-now quarterbacks either. No returning dignitaries of any kind. I believe that this is a problem for all five thousand of us here in Little Falls, this forgotten chunk of earth in upstate New York. We could all use a good parade, a fund-raiser, something where we could stand to the side and lie about the ways and degrees in which we violated the famous in our youth. Who we fucked standing up, who we beat the absolute-living-hell out of, who we out-drank and then left laid out in their own vomit. All we want is the chance to do violence to our old classmates' bodies and to their reputations. Maybe tear down their *Welcome Home* banners.

Other towns have their opportunities. I went to a parade in Herkimer last year. A soap-opera star home for Fourth of July. He was a big, good-looking guy with a California tan. His name is Chip and you've seen him. He's as famous as famous gets. As Chip eased by on the town's favorite-son convertible, an old boy in front of me said, "A goddamned queer. Remember? Remember him and Boyle outside the art room?"

"Remember?" his buddy said in gleeful mock outrage. "I was there to beat the shit out of the both of them."

By God, that's what we need. Someone to hate from great distances of time and space and social circles. A politician, someone who wants to be one, anything.

As it stands, we're left with each other. This is what I'm here to tell you downstaters and outsiders who have your pick of scapegoats and enemies and hated rising stars. Up here, we don't have those kinds of choices. We're stuck wounding the people we know in all the familiar, vicious ways. It's not something we can help.

I am also here to tell you that we hurt each other so badly because of our jobs, because of who does what, for how much, and for how long. Me, I'm a school teacher. Ninth-grade English, to be exact. My wife, Sabrina, is a dental hygienist, a hard job I'm sure, and one I don't like to think about. The reason is, once a year Sabrina makes me come in for a cleaning and she's a changed person in that room, I swear. She wears a protective mask, a face-length visor. I tell her she looks like a welder in that thing and that is exactly the way she acts: like a person possessed by the charm of dangerous machinery. The fact that she lives in people's mouths just complicates things. Her sort of oral violence doesn't sit well with me, necessary or not.

"Open up," she tells me while I'm in the chair. "Spit." These are commands, not requests. What kind of way is that for two married people to talk? That's not the way it works at home, believe it, but at work anything goes.

"Your mouth is a disaster," Sabrina says.

"That's an awful thing to say," I tell her.

"I'm just doing my job," she claims, and I believe she is right. You see what I mean? You see how work can ruin people? You see why we need someone with a world, a job beyond the scope of our own, someone who will come home and let us feel up their livelihood and smile and wave and pretend that they don't know it's happening?

It takes two whole weeks after a routine cleaning for my wife and me to be in love again.

I'm telling you all this because of what happened two weeks ago, Friday, July 29, when we had people over to dinner, and when my ideas about work turned from theory to practice to disaster. There were four people coming over to our house that night, two couples, people Sabrina and I knew pretty well. Michael and Celene were and are doctors, one a pathologist and one an obstetrician. And then Sid and Lori: ex-high-school math teacher and real-estate agent, respectively. Sid quit teaching two years ago, citing burnout, and hasn't found another job since. Sid also drinks, heavily, although Lori does not drink at all. She does have a good temper, though, and a nice way of dealing privately with public problems. To be true, I find this quality plenty endearing. Lori is a woman who knows that life, at its core, is embarrassing.

As for Michael and Celene, they don't do much except for work, although they do play tennis. They make a big deal out of this, playing tennis every Saturday morning. It's their quality time, the rock-solid basis to their marriage. They're not afraid to publicize it.

Sabrina is neutral about which couple she likes better, but I prefer Sid and Lori, something she can't understand.

"Why do you have to like one more than the other?" she says. "What is your thing with having favorites?"

"It's not that I have to like one more than the other. I just do. I just happen to like Sid and Lori better. There is no compulsion involved here. And I like Sid the best out of everyone. That doesn't make it a political choice."

"But you're a teacher," she says. "You're supposed to be neutral."

I laugh at that one every time. "There is a kid in my lower-level section," I tell her. "Every time I turn around to the board, he punches the girl next to him in the side of the head. He hits her with a closed fist. How neutral should I feel about that little asshole?"

Still, I like Michael and Celene fine. "They're both perfectly nice people," I told Sabrina the night before they came over for dinner.

And it's true: they are perfectly nice people. But it is also true that I had been in a bad way in the days and weeks leading up to that dinner. For one, it was my summer vacation, and I'd been doing some drinking. This doesn't make me much different from most people; it's just that my summer vacation lasts the whole summer and not a week or two weeks or anything remotely human like that. No surprise, this is also when I start thinking about the people I know, about what they do for a living and what they don't do. This kind of speculation helps pass incredible amounts of time, especially in late July, the belly of my vacation, when a life of leisure wears thin in places you can't begin to imagine.

"Listen to this jerk-off," my working friends always say when I complain about all my free time. Around mid-July they become consumed with the thought of their week-long August vacations and their neglected Criscraft outboards and their Lake Placid time-shares and their rural white-boy *Field and Stream* dreams of the good life. They listen to me complaining and spin off into some new lower middle-class orbit of righteousness. "Three months of vacation and he's bitching. What kind of job is it you have anyway? You call what you do *work?* And it's people like me who are paying your salary. I pay taxes. You're fired."

And so on. My out-of-work friends, like Sid, have no such complaints. They're just happy to have someone around in the middle of the day, someone they can call at noon on a Tuesday and ask, "What's going on?" and someone who will answer, "Nothing." My out-of-work friends have almost no interest in putting me on the defensive. They're ecstatic that they're not alone for once, that someone isn't shitting on them with their salt-of-the-earth routine.

What I'm saying is that I was in a truly susceptible frame of mind the day of our dinner party. I could make excuses and say that the dinner was a matter of bad timing, that if it had been a week later everything would have been fine. I could say that July is just a bad month for me, flat out, with its surplus of free time and beer and heat. That I'm just not a July person. In fact, I have said these things. I have also said, "I'm sorry," repeatedly. To this, Sabrina responds, "Don't be a goddamn liar, Gerald."

There is no good comeback to this. I *am* sorry, but it's also true that I am, on occasion, a liar. It is my lying that started all our troubles, a fact that makes Sabrina's request so difficult to ignore.

Anyway, the six of us sat down at our backyard picnic table that night, and all was fine at first—the shish kabob was good, the conversation friendly—and we were into our second bottle of wine and having an early go at drunkenness when Michael asked Sid: "So, how's the job search going?"

Sid was chewing a piece a meat and finished chewing before saying to Michael: "Nothing new, nothing big."

"That's really too bad. It's unbelievable, really. What kind of things are you looking for?"

"Well, I'm looking at different things. What I'd really like to do is work with my hands. You know, something that will keep me busy, make me tired. A good tired, is what I'm saying, not just a mental tired."

The truth was that Sid wasn't looking at all and Michael should have known that. He should have known by the way Sid spoke that this wasn't a conversation that interested him. Work or talking about work, particularly his own, wasn't high on his list of things to do. And it's not that Michael was a bastard about the whole thing. He was just a little dense, which is not as bad as being mean-spirited, but is just as dangerous.

"Really?" Michael said. He seemed interested now. He dropped the fork he'd been holding and raised his glass of wine to his mouth. "What kind of work are you thinking about, exactly? I mean there are all kinds of things you might do."

"I've got an eye out for carpentry jobs. I've done some general construction and that wasn't so bad. I could do that. But carpentry is the way I think I'll go."

That was as good a place to end the conversation as any. Sid set it up that way, and we all saw it, I think, except for Michael. He had an eye-shine that said: "I'd like to help you." He wasn't in any mood to be subtle. He was busy being philanthropic.

"So where are you looking? I mean, what kind of channels are you going through?" Michael clearly directed these questions at Sid, but it was Lori who answered.

"You know, Sid and I decided that we're too old to go rushing into things. I mean, Jesus we're not that old, but we are particular. We can wait out the good jobs. I get the inside track on all the contracting and development news through my office. The big and the small stuff. Something will come up, and there isn't much use thinking about it until it does."

There was a pause and Sabrina took the opportunity with both fists.

"Would anyone like more food? Wine? Celene, you look like you could use a little more."

Celene did want more wine, said so, and so Sabrina poured her some. In fact, everyone wanted some. This was as pure a diversionary tactic as I've ever seen, and for a few seconds it worked. Those few seconds were the crucial time. I probably should have said something. Something to move the conversation. As the host, that was my job. I should have been a neutralizing force. But why just me? Why not anyone else? We all gave Michael another chance to push things too far.

"You know, there is something to be said about patience," Michael went on. "Patience is a good thing. But on the other hand, sometimes you have to go out and get things. You can't just wait for them. Sometimes that's the worst thing you can do."

Michael's voice had changed slightly. It sounded like he had a job and wanted to know why anybody couldn't get one. I heard it and I'm sure Sid heard it too, both of us being sensitive to these types of things. Sabrina claimed later that she didn't hear, but she did think that Michael was pushing things a little too far. This means she heard, and could admit to it only in code.

And maybe Michael himself knew that he had pushed things too far, because he gave a little embarrassed laugh and said: "Well, you could always go back to teaching. That's not exactly backbreaking work anyway, is it."

This was clearly a joke. I knew that. But still, I got myself into a little fit of resentment and said: "Wait a minute."

"Come on, Gerald," Sabrina said. "I've heard you say the exact same thing."

And I have, it's true. I've often said that we teachers don't *work,* exactly. What we do is plan, budget. We section off the day into seven, fifty-minute periods. We take ten periods of material and turn it into fifteen. For instance, I can stretch out *Julius Caesar* for eleven periods. That's five hundred and fifty minutes, not counting attendance, which I tend to drag out like an acceptance speech. Five hundred and fifty minutes may be more than *Julius Caesar* needs, but it is a testament to my ability to make things—time, literature—work for me.

I wouldn't say I work, then; I would say I do a kind of simple math for a living. I am a mostly well-intentioned, highly educated bean counter. Nonetheless, I didn't like Michael joking about my job one bit, no matter how true the joke was. So I turned against him somewhat, and even found myself *hating* Michael a little, when Sid took a sip of wine and asked, "So, Michael, who was that you were with the other day when I saw you?"

"Who was who?"

"That woman you were with the other day. You were coming out of the hospital with her, and I waved, but you didn't see me."

Which was a lie. I know it was a lie because Sid would never have waved to Michael. He doesn't know him well enough; in fact, Sid and Michael only knew each other through me, and weren't really friends at all. In Sid's mind, they didn't have that kind of relationship, the kind where you would flag someone down from great distances. Michael, not operating by these rules of social reservation, couldn't have known that, but I did. I knew Sid wasn't anywhere near the hospital, and I knew he didn't see Michael there, companion or not.

"I'm not sure when you're talking about," Michael said.

"It was the other day. I think it was Tuesday, although it might have been Wednesday. I think she might have been another doctor."

"Why do you say that? Was she wearing a lab coat or something?"

"She may have, but I'm not too sure. I can remember just thinking that she looked like a doctor, if that makes any sense."

It was obvious that Sid was having a good time at this point, but the conversation hadn't gone far enough to make the rest of us uncomfortable. At this moment, we just wanted to know where it was all going and how it was going to be resolved. There is intrigue in unraveling these mysteries of mutual acquaintances, and we waited for them to arrive at the right name, the right place and time.

I shouldn't use the word "we" so easily. Celene was probably already uncomfortable. She knew where this might be going. Her face said that this was old, familiar territory.

"Maybe it was Lynn Karpath," Celene said, turning to her husband.

"No, I don't think it was Dr. Karpath. I haven't seen her lately. Or in a while, for that matter." Michael's voice was jerky, like it was caught on something. It was a small thing but we all could hear it. He asked for more wine, and Sabrina poured him some.

Celene looked away from her husband and over at Sid. She asked him, "This woman. Did she have blonde hair?"

"Yes, she did."

"Was she my height, maybe a little taller?"

"A little taller. Yeah, I think that's right. Not too much taller though. Maybe an inch." Sid thought about it for a second. "Two inches at most," he said.

"It sounds like Lynn Karpath to me," Celene said.

"Well, it must be her then. I'm glad we figured this out." I looked over at Sid. He didn't seem like he was having fun anymore. He looked serious, like he was willing to take things where they shouldn't go.

Michael and Celene were sitting next to each other on one bench, Sid and Lori doing the same on the opposite side of the table. Sabrina and I sat at the ends in white plastic chairs. Michael turned all the way around to face Celene, his legs straddling the bench. In a deadly serious voice he said, "Celene, I don't care what Sid says he saw. I wasn't walking with Lynn Karpath. If it was her he saw, then it wasn't me she was walking with. If it was me, it wasn't her."

If you've ever heard someone tell the truth, you would know that Michael was telling it at that moment. His voice was clear, each consonant, each vowel sure of its own purity. It was a kind of voice you wouldn't challenge if you were at all interested in honesty.

"You know, Michael, I think I saw you with someone like that the other day, too. It wasn't exactly in front of the hospital, but it was near there."

I don't know exactly why I said it, and the reasons I have probably aren't good enough to mention. I should have just let them settle it. It should have stayed something between Sid and Michael and Michael and Celene. Let's just say I don't know why I did it. Let's just say it slipped, and that I would take it back if retraction were still a possibility. If that isn't good enough, let's just say I felt like I was involved already. Staying out of it didn't seem to be an option.

Without moving, Michael looked at me and said, "You know you are a fucking liar. You've got to know that. There can't be any doubt in your mind that you are a conscienceless fucking liar."

With that, Sid came over the table at Michael. It was something he had been waiting to do, although I suspect that Sid doesn't really hate Michael, doesn't even dislike him. The circumstances were right. There were strange, unspoken things going between the three of us, forces that made us do what we did. I'd like to think that things were beyond our control, although Sabrina claims that this is so much garbage, and I have to admit that she's probably right.

By the time I got in there to break it up, Sid was kneeling on the table and he had Michael bent over backward. Michael's legs were stuck somehow underneath the bench. In that position, Sid was obviously getting the better of it. He had all the advantages of leverage and gravity. When I tried to separate them, I somehow got caught up in the flaying limbs, the push-and-pull of things, and we all fell to the ground. I threw a few punches while we were there on the grass, and got hit by a few.

The blows were soft-sounding, muffled, as if we weren't really hitting each other but plastic dolls made to look like us. The women were yelling, but other than that, noise seemed to have lost its ability to have any real effect upon the three of us.

We stopped fighting when Michael got hold of a salad bowl and hit Sid over the head with it. The bowl was ceramic and it shattered on impact, but not before making an unmistakable sound. The sound was loud, a resounding crack. It was a sound that tells you when a fight is about to become something irreversible, something settled not by mutual consent but by hospitals, lawyers, by the people who love you and their lifelong grudges.

I lay there for a second and watched everyone get their things together and leave. Sid was bleeding badly from his forehead. It was something he should have gone to the hospital for, but I have no way of knowing if he did. We haven't talked to or seen each other since. I think we're afraid to see each other, as if seeing each other might be a kind of confession in itself. He and Lori left, and Michael and Celene followed them a minute later. Michael somehow remembered to take the casserole dish they had brought over. It might be the only intact thing they left with that night. I don't know. I haven't spoken to any of them, and that's too bad. They are all decent people, as far as decency goes.

Sabrina and I sat outside for a while that night. The sun went down while we sat there, and the air turned cool, too cool for what we were wearing. Sabrina got up once to get sweatshirts for both of us and ice for my right eye, which was swelling from the fight. When she went inside and when she came back out, the motion light came on, spooking me like it always does. I remember looking up into that light and watching the bugs swarm there, diving into and in front of the bulb's eye. I wondered how they managed to get there so quickly, if they waited there in the dark for hours, just for the chance to do what they were supposed to. Those bugs were opportunists. God knows what they wanted from that light or why they wanted it, but at the very least they were in the right positions to get at it first.

What happens when one bug gets what another one doesn't? I

wondered that night. What happens then? I suspect I already know the answer. It isn't what you would call a taxing question.

That night, we sat there in the dark for three hours before we finally went to bed. This was before Sabrina began to blame me for that night, before she bothered to figure out how and why things happened as they did. As I applied ice to my eye, she sat there with her hand on my leg. She moved the hand a couple of times, and once she wiped her face as if she were crying, but mostly we just sat there, watching and listening to our backyard negotiate its sleep with the nighttime.

I remember asking myself that night: What can you count on? It seemed like an important question, and I thought about for it a long time. What matters? I thought, listing the things that people normally rely upon: their jobs, their friends, their cars, and their connections. I wanted to do away with all of that, to rid myself of all the lousy things of this world. I wanted to reduce life to its bare bones. What do you really need? Ultimately, I decided on Sabrina's hand. It was heavy on my leg, unmoving, and its weight was reassuring. It reminded me of how the best things in this life are supposed to be simple. What else do I need besides this hand on my leg? I asked myself. What else is there?

Sabrina moved the hand, obviously, put it right in her pocket. I suppose she got cold; or maybe she just moved beyond sad, into the place where you break down emotions in terms of who made them public property. Whatever, the hand was moved. I asked Sabrina to put it back on my leg and she did, but it wasn't the same, and when she stuffed her hand back in her pocket a few minutes later, I didn't object.

We sat for a while longer that night, not touching, not speaking, until finally Sabrina asked, "Why can't we be better people? What won't we do to hurt each other?" She didn't look at me, like she was addressing the sky, the house, the motion light, but it was clear whose questions they were to answer.

Those two questions have stayed with me. It's August now, only three weeks until school begins, and there are still no parades scheduled, no rich-and-famous coming home just to place themselves at our collective mercy. No clear shot at someone who is above the fray. And other than that, I still haven't come up with the answers to Sabrina's questions. But I want to be a better person, I do, and so I will keep trying to find those answers. Besides, I don't have much to do until school starts in September anyway—and as everyone knows, being a teacher isn't exactly backbreaking work in the first place—and so even if I haven't found the answers when school begins, I will keep trying.

The
Right Questions

I'm with my wife, Mary Kay, and her ex-husband, Scoot, and we're crouched behind a row of evergreen bushes waiting for my father to take out his trash naked. This is my father's thing. You call him, and he brings his trash out for you, and you watch. I've done the calling and watching for nine years, mostly when I am drunk and mean-spirited. I've hooted, I'll admit. Thrown a beer can or two, some a little short of empty. I've taken great pleasure in his comparatively low place in life. But I never knew he was my father until two months ago. Now, instead of sitting out in my 1981 Chevy Monte Carlo, honking and whooping at my father's private parts, I'm hiding in the bushes in front of his red-brick ranch house, shivering in the cold October wind blowing off the Adirondacks. Meanwhile, my wife and her ex-husband are hashing out old times. Scoot is an Army sergeant, on leave, and he's also the manufacturer of pornographic novelty items. He has just offered Mary Kay a key chain. I distrust Scoot's motives as an ex-husband, and so I sneak a quick look at what's written on the plastic tab of the key chain. I do not like what I see.

"Hey, now," I say.

"Look here," Scoot tells Mary Kay. "It says 'Wine Me, Dine Me, Sixty-Nine Me.'"

"I can read," she says.

I tell you, it's a strange goddamn world.

How we all got to the here and now is a long tale worthy of a few sighs and gasps and maybe a good, fierce wail, but first you should know the following: in 1970, when I was three years old, my mother told me that my father was dead in the Vietnam War. I believed her, because plenty of fathers were. Most of those fathers came back in pieces of bone and flesh and brains, stuffed in boxes or jars or spread out on government paper or run through the chop shop of rumor. Not my father. It turns out that he never left Little Falls. My mother, her lips loosened by the threat of the great beyond, told me on her death-bed that we've lived in the same town for twenty-five years. Now my father is no longer a dead soldier. Instead, he is Larry Fouchard, an exhibitionist, a celebrity in this lonely part of upstate New York.

Now that I know, I wish my father were more like other fathers.

It is true that this violent world loves a warrior—Geronimo, General MacArthur, John Wayne, and the like—and as a youth I was no worse than most people. That is, I rooted for the Republicans versus the Democrats, the Dallas Cowboys versus the Pittsburgh Steelers, and reveled in the character-building mayhem that is Pop Warner football. My mother never talked about my father, and I barely thought about him, except to remember that he was dead and vaguely heroic. But my V.F.W. desires began for real when I was sixteen. That's when I started pumping gas at John's Service Station. I was the kind of boy genius that teachers and Rotarians were always disappointed in: the sort who could memorize the wordplay of old Mercutio and Tybalt, but would fail at addition, penmanship, and normal human communication. Still, I never expected to be pumping gas. Slaving at the gas station is one thing you rule out for yourself in life, although you always reserve the possibility for others. At one point I had all my sworn enemies in my dreams working at a gas station, sweating all over my car and then apologizing. I was giving them tips. When I woke up I was sixteen, employed part-time at John's Service Station, smelling the gasoline on my fingertips when no one was looking, thinking about the fast track to a management position, which I got on and rode. That was me. You've never met a man so driven. I was in love with fossil fuels.

When you are sixteen, sneaking back behind the gas station, pouring gasoline all over your hands out of a dinged red can with no spout, you start suspecting that you've gone a long way toward proving your own failure. But instead of quitting, I stepped back, made myself a martial legacy from the TV. I didn't need my father before, but now I was dressing him up like some dummy, sometimes in Union blues, no cap, sometimes Spartacus in a thong, always sweating his sorry trail across the jungle, always proving my worth with his own. By the time I was a high school senior, he was accepting the surrender of Cornwallis, wearing high boots and epaulets. At that point I was scared of war, but also afraid to look scared of it. So I walked the hallways of my school wearing Members Only jackets with loops at the shoulders. I affected the demeanor of a tattoo-wearer. Sometimes I scowled.

That was before I finally tuned-in to the twentieth century. Patton was liberating the Italians. I looked at myself. I was wearing chintz. Patton didn't wear chintz.

But it didn't matter. I went to school with the children of dairy farmers, paper mill workers, bank tellers, and beauticians, and whatever likeness I had to these heirs to our sorry piece of the failing old world, in my mind my dead father meant that I was something different and better than all of them. This was especially true at the gas station, where Patton's Italians still needed saving, mostly from themselves. I'm talking about my good friends Bummer and Bennie Marchetti, who worked at the gas station with me. Their father owned the station, and Bummer in particular hated Mr. Marchetti for his low pay-scale, see-through dress shirts, and spit-shined Lucchese boots. One day, Bummer came in and said he had a plan to kill all the Italians. He said they were all style, no substance. This pissed off Bummer to the point of genocide. "I'll kill them, all right," he promised me.

"Your last name is Marchetti," I said. I reminded him that he was Italian all the way through. But Bummer insisted he was Austrian, which means that he wished he were Austrian. I laughed at him. I'm not laughing now.

"It's true," he said. "Sometimes you can't tell the difference between the Italians and the Austrians. Hell, sometimes they can't even tell the difference. They're from the same—what is it?—*tribe.*"

"They're not from any tribe," I told him. "Why can't you just be Italian? What are you trying to prove?"

This burned him up. "It's no choice," he said. "It's all in the goddamn blood."

Then Bennie, who is older than Bummer by one year and bigger by fifty pounds, started screaming Bummer's name, repeatedly. In Rome, the cardinals pick their pope by yelling out his name all at once. It's called *acclamation.* Anyway, that's what Bennie told us. He said he was picking Bummer to be an Italian. Bummer said fine, he'd be an Italian if Bennie stopped screaming. Which he did.

The point is that I knew that Bummer and Bennie were both insane, and that I was not insane because of my father, who was a bit of a war hero and who was not cheap or alive or Italian. And Bummer, Bennie, and I knew we were all better off than the son of Larry Fouchard, if there was one. This was about the time I started paying my visits to Larry's house, although I had heard of him long before. He was a legend in the town, and like most of our small-town legends, no one knew where he came from, what income he lived on, or why he did what he did. No one really wanted to know. But nearly every graduating senior at the Little Falls Jr.-Sr. High School had done the coldhearted thing I'm about to describe. Larry lived only a half-mile away from my and my mother's own red-brick ranch house. On the night the Italian race was threatened with extinction, Bummer, Bennie, and I went to my house after work. My mother was working late at her bookkeeping job down at the Mohawk Valley Paper Co., and while she was gone, the three of us drank her twelve-pack of Utica Club beer, and rang up Larry. Then we drove over to his house, honked our horn, and threw our beer cans while my father—with his gray hair, slightly-curved spine, and sad wrinkled body and body parts—brought his garbage to the curb and then walked back to his house. He stood in his doorway silently and pathetically while we spoke all the profound truths that can be contained within the words "fuck" and "shit" and their various combinations. Then we lay a whole lot of squeal and little rubber out in front of my poor father's house, just to let him see that we knew the ideals of joy and freedom, while he was stuck with the dregs of heartache and hopelessness. By the time we were through, the Marchetti brothers were feeling pretty good about their father, and so was I.

You see what I'm saying here? Some people love their parents, some don't. That's easy. I never loved my father, but I loved the idea of him. Now that he's real, I wonder what that makes me. I used to think that my father could tell me something about myself. Now I'm scared that he already has.

My mother was different. When she was real I loved her, but the idea of her gives me night sweats. From what she told me, my mother didn't love my father but saw him naked on the lawn in the fall of 1966, and wanted him. She brought him over a six-pack of tall boys, cold. He didn't want the beer, but my mother did and she drank all of it and then wanted my father even more. My father had my mother once, but didn't want her more than that and told her so. He told her he didn't know what he wanted.

"Who does know what they want?" my mother asked him.

"No idea," my father said. "Lyndon Johnson. Or maybe God."

God I don't really believe in, although he still scares me. My mother believed in God. She was too scared not to. That's why when she was dying of breast cancer at the age of fifty-four, she broke down and she told me all that I'm telling you: told me that my father was not in fact dead in Vietnam, not dead at all, no veteran. "I am wary of my eternal reward," she said. "And virtue demands the truth. Bradley, you are the only son of Larry Fouchard."

We were in the Little Falls Memorial Hospital. My mother was in bed. It was a death scene common to soap operas and the imaginations of young, suicidal romantics, and I get an ache in the heart region just thinking about it. My mother's face was thin with grief, pain, and honest parental love, and I knew she was telling the truth. But I pretended that she wasn't.

"It's all right, Mom," I told her, patting her arm. "You're not making much sense, but that's fine because you're a little sick."

"I'm dying."

I had no good response to this. It was another truth.

"Do you hear me, Bradley?" she said. "I'm dying and I'm telling you that your father is Larry Fouchard. And Larry knows that you are his son. I told him so myself a week after you were born."

Friends, the question you might want answered here is: What did it feel like to face all these hard facts? Go do the following: climb in your car and find yourself a highway. Get your vehicle up to an honest cruising speed—sixty-five or seventy. Then open the door, and abandon car. Land on your stomach. Hit a sign post if you can. Say hello to the guard rail. Chew a little gravel. Bounce your head off the pavement a few dozen times, just so you lose your sense of what's good and right in the world.

It hurt worse than that.

But I knew right then that things would have to change, that I would have to start asking the tough questions if life was to make sense again. So I asked my mother why she did what she did.

"Be specific," she said. "I've done lots of things."

"Why did you lie to me?"

"I was afraid," she said.

"You're afraid now."

"That's true," she said. Then, for the last time, my mother reminded me how life used to be and how it would be from now on and how life was something I might want to be afraid of. She explained that she was not one of those born liars, but only a liar born of circumstance. She had a son, but no presentable father, so she made one up and pretty soon had him dying all over the country of Vietnam. And if you're that son, you believe it. If you're the mother, she said, you start believing it, too. You live your life thinking you're special, but never for the right reasons. Then you learn the truth.

"The truth," my mother said, "is the thing you never admit to until it's too late."

She died two days later.

The truth hurt so much that I went out and got married. I had known Mary Kay for two years. We met one Thursday night at the Happen Inn, where I was dancing with a pool cue the way Fred did not dance with Ginger. I was all limb and spasm, showing off moves favored by professional wrestlers and Catholics at charismatic masses. I was completing one fantastic spin when I elbowed Mary Kay in the collarbone on her way to the bathroom.

"Easy," she said. "You're going to hurt somebody."

"I'm going to hurt myself," I told her.

"I believe it," she said.

Then she smiled and did not continue on to the bathroom.

This was love, folks, the kind of love that cannot be compared to expensive flowers or Caribbean sunsets or white hot flame. No, this was a love blind to the mechanics of social status and financial well-being, a love mindful of physical urges and beauty hidden in the smaller details. This was the kind of love that caused me to call Mary Kay at the community college, where she was a part-time, overnight switchboard operator, just so I could hear the hum and purr of her voice in the early morning. We had what the understated among us like to call "a good thing."

We had such a good thing that the day after my mother died, I asked Mary Kay to marry me. We were married the day after that. I thought marriage might help. When you are married you share your misery, which is what everyone says marriage is about, which makes you wonder about its attraction as a lifelong institution. But who am I? I am making my wife miserable.

The husband who made her miserable before me was Scoot, which brings this story a little closer to where it's headed. Before Scoot went into the Army, before he left Mary Kay, he was a professional baseball player. Scoot played for two years in Toledo, where he reached a point of no advancement. After two years, Scoot told Mary Kay that he had lost his bearing altogether, that he had no sense of what went where anymore. It got so bad that one day, he stepped back and said to Mary Kay: "Toledo." He had no idea whether Toledo was in Ohio or Kentucky or some other state altogether. Mary Kay says it wasn't a matter of forgetting—Scoot just didn't know.

At that time in history there was a bumper sticker popular around the Toledo area that said: "Ohio is a State of Mind." Mary Kay bought one for Scoot, but he said it didn't help him any. "Where in the hell am I?" he asked her.

Finally Scoot told Mary Kay that he felt dulled-out. "I am too distant from the cut-and-paste of the mind," he said. So Scoot left her to join the Army. The Army sent him to Germany, where he discovered that as a shortstop he possessed limited range, but as a man had a generous sense of vulgarity. Scoot found that there were Germans who liked their Americana with an edge, so he opened up a dirty T-shirt shop on the side. He sends snapshots of himself with his products to Mary Kay. In one picture Scoot is standing next to a truck with a bug guard that says, "CROTCH CLIMBER" in a western script. In another, he's wearing a T-shirt that reads "Happiness is a Tight Pussy!" With each picture there is a note—"Wiesbaden, June, 1986," "Hamburg, October, 1987"—and then his signature contained within a hand-drawn red heart. The stationary is Army issue. We've got a whole album of this stuff.

You would think that next to Scoot, I'd look pretty good as a life-partner. This was probably true for a while. But to be honest, I've been less of a man since learning that I spent the last nine years worshipping the fake father, persecuting the real one. And even worse, that the fake father was probably only a dirty old soldier like Scoot, and that the real one is Larry Fouchard. All this cruel human behavior and historical revision left a real strain on my marriage. After the first five weeks of married life, I was still sitting around the house, drinking beer, listening to my own sour heart. Finally Mary Kay said, "Change your life or something." She wanted me to pray. She was praying and said I should, too. I had abandoned religion as a teenager, and had no idea who to pray to, but she said that it didn't matter, just so long as I believed in belief. She told me I could pray to the dog and it wouldn't be better or worse than anything else in the world. So I started praying to the dog. It is a nice, old yellow Lab with some bad arthritis in its front legs. I prayed to the dog that my father was not really Larry Fouchard.

"Old Pal," I told it, "when You stop limping, I'll know my prayers have been answered." I prayed to the mutt every morning as he straggled outside to go and relieve himself. Sometimes he even went lying down, his old legs were so rotten. "Sit up and piss, Old Pal," I said. "I have faith that You will."

When Mary Kay found out that I was actually praying to the dog and not to a divine abstraction, she began making threatening sounds deep in her throat. Her eyes were dark blue and murderous. "Heaven has no place for the literal minded," she said, as if it were my last chance to prove myself human, whatever that is.

What is my problem? Why am I such a bad person? Why am I such a bad husband? You don't see Mary Kay calling in sick to work, staying in bed until two in the afternoon, wondering about a world that gives you two choices in husbands and both of them bad. What exactly is the difference between she and I, wife and husband? When I asked her this, Mary Kay let go of the pain of our five married weeks together. She said that I was too scared to be good, that I was too perverse to be better. She told me that I let myself be a victim of history. What kind of man is it, she asked, that lets the dead father he does not know define the man that he is? What kind of man uses this nonexistent father to redeem all of his failures and lost potential? What kind of man spends his entire semi-adult life hassling and torturing his real father? And what kind of man does not even apologize to the real father once the truth about him is known? What kind?

"At one time," Mary Kay said sadly, "I thought you were handsome and brooding. But sooner or later self-hate turns into a gut and sags and gets ugly."

Mary Kay paused, and took a deep, meaningful breath.

"And let me tell you, Bradley," Mary Kay said. "You have turned a little ugly."

Mary Kay must have noticed my face cracking and breaking in the morning kitchen light, because her fierce stare softened somewhat and her body slouched a little. She sat awhile and sighed repeatedly.

"Everyone has something to learn from the past," Mary Kay eventually told me, straight out. "Learn something."

I thought about what Mary Kay said about me and history, and I realized it was the truth. But I was still afraid to confront my father. So I tried to learn something about the past in a different way, which means I signed up for a history class at the community college. I got there, and the teacher had on an eye patch. He had lost the eye in the Argonne and said he knew tragedy of all kinds. Instead of showing us a picture of Queen Elizabeth, he took off his patch. "Look upon the Queen of the Renaissance," he said, showing us his withered socket. "Her sour puss courts metaphor."

He gave me hope. I had heard of people making good things out of bad. So I walked up to him after class.

"Sure," I said to him. "Your weakness is your strength. Your eye is a way of explaining the past."

"My eye," he said, "is a figure of speech." Then he raised his nose at me, not like I smelled, but like I was a smell.

It turns out that the history class was not what Mary Kay had in mind. But she agreed that I was a smell for going to the class in the first place, and not having it out with my father. Once you find out that you are a smell, you become a good study of your own disaster. And the lesson here is: Fuck the past, that is, unless you're in it. Never admit that you didn't exist. Define history in relation to yourself. But it never works. History always comes back, not to tell you why bad things happen, but why you deserve them.

As you know, old Scoot came back the way ex-husbands do, endlessly. This was yesterday. He was home on leave, wearing his uniform, and talking up the intersections of business and brain work. "I deal in world views," he told Mary Kay. "My mind is expansive. Profitable, too." I was in the backyard, explaining to Old Pal that failure makes you small, and would he forgive me. Mary Kay doesn't suffer fools gladly. She probably knew that ex-husbands come back only to talk about what went wrong, and how things might be right again. She had no use for Scoot standing around the kitchen, intellectualizing the moral ruin of their marriage. So when she saw me talking to the dog, Mary Kay sent Scoot right out. She gave that sick bastard a beer, but he wasn't sharing.

"The awkward thing about praying to your dog," he said, coming up behind me, "is that the dog will die, and if you care about its afterlife—and you will—then you'll find yourself praying both *for* the dog and *to* the dog. This is a problem."

"It's the same problem with Jesus Christ," I pointed out. "One foot in both worlds."

Scoot sat down next to me on the picnic table bench and lit up a cigarette. He blew smoke at me through his nose and flung in one more time.

"I wouldn't pray to that dog. It'll go nowhere. Into the void."

"Sure," I said, "You hate dogs."

"Hating or not hating," he said, "dogs lack souls. Heaven can't use them."

He had me there. I felt like I had lost something: a bet, a pen, my life.

"Get used to it," Scoot said. "It's a mystery of the divine. Not that a dog does not have a soul, but that someone can tell him he lacks one. Back on earth, we call this a law."

I shrugged. "You're pretty smart for a pervert," I told him.

This got to him. He shrunk some and then went off on a coughing jag. When he came back he admitted, "It's true. Wants are my one thing."

"Wants were my mother's one thing, too," I told him. I could have kept him on the hook, but what I wanted was the comfort of empathy. So I let loose with the whole story, which only cheered him up. He was feeling pretty good about life when I got through with him. "I've got a problem," he said, "But what you've got is a condition."

Scoot then got up and went out to his pickup truck, where I

imagined he had something else to torture me with: old pictures of he and Mary Kay, steamy love letters, startling new theories about life and how not to live it. Instead, he came back with a case of warm beer and some advice. This surprised me, coming from a man whom I believed to be morally suspect, plus possibly coveting my wife.

"Don't be so shocked," he said. "We've got more in common than you think. We're just two men, wrestling with our problems and with our two dumb, hurting hearts."

It turns out that Scoot has his own father to worry about. His father, Scoot told me, retired last year at the age of fifty-five and became a drunk. He took up swearing. He menaced daytime game-show hosts from his easy chair. He rolled three different cars on the way to high school basketball games. Finally, Scoot's mother threatened to put him through the slow roast of divorce. "Once you're alone, your life will be over," she told him. Scoot's mother and all their friends sat him down. They went around in a circle and each one told Scoot's father the ways in which he disgusted them. "We hate you," they told him.

Scoot's father stopped drinking.

"All he needed," Scoot told me, "was a healthy dose of realism."

That night, after Scoot had gone to sleep and I was in bed with Mary Kay, I said to myself: Bradley, this is a situation that calls for realism. Let's be realistic about the world and those who live in it. Like most folks on this cold patch of earth, I was taught the Bible as a child, and am familiar with the story of Ham, who saw his daddy, Noah, drunk and naked, and was banished. So being real, I admitted that I was a Ham to my father's Noah, except not knowing he was a father, let alone mine, not just seeing him naked once but whenever I wanted. Then I stopped being real and started in drinking again. At two in the morning, I woke up Scoot and told him realism wasn't working for me.

"Fuck you," he said. "Go to sleep and try it again tomorrow."

When I woke up, I was still drunk, but gave it another go. Drunk, I remembered that it was me always drunk and not my father. Ashamed, I remembered that not only is my father not drunk, but he is not ashamed either, proud to be naked on his front lawn, carrying out his garbage, happy that anyone who needs to see him can. Before I gave up realism for dead, I realized my father does some damn good work. He's a rock. I've seen him during rainstorms, weekends, blue-balled at Christmas. Right then, I admitted for the first time that it is my father, Larry Fouchard, who has every reason to be ashamed of me, his son.

Ham saw Noah and lost the keys to the kingdom. I wonder what I've lost.

Scoot slept in this morning, and I was settling in for the long haul, thinking about quitting my job, thinking about quitting life. Mary Kay looked at me sadly and whispered in my ear, "Enough." She brought me a pad and a pencil and said I should make a list.

"A list," I said back to her.

"A list of the things to like about your father. Something to build on."

So I made a list. Things to like about my father:

A sense of the mystery of being. My mother told me he was "a riddle wrapped in an enigma."

A seriousness of purpose. Picture the president on TV, ashen-faced, telling you about bomb shelters, tax breaks, all the things you need to know.

Stage presence. My father has a floodlight on the corner of his garage. The time to see him is at night. He sure knows how to work that floodlight.

Tendentiousness.

Absolute fearlessness.

Style.

I filled up two pages right there. I had hope.

"Great," Mary Kay said. "Now the flip side."

I made another list.

A life easily reduced to a series of dick jokes.

A vulnerability to dramatic swings in weather, fashion, popular morality.

Loneliness.

Loneliness.

Loneliness.

I was finishing up the list at one this afternoon when Scoot came downstairs. He asked to read the list and I gave it to him. My attempt at redemption touched him some, and he grew a little teary. He poured himself some coffee and told Mary Kay and me the rest of the story about his father. Once Scoot's father stopped drinking, Scoot told us, he went back to work. He also stopped talking to his wife, his friends, everybody. This, Scoot explained, is a killer. So Scoot's mother has started drinking. She's even started going to high school basketball games, where she sits by herself and gets on this one player, a not-so aggressive point guard named Jerry. "C'mon Jere," she yells at this poor kid during timeouts. "You gotta want that thing."

When she sobers up, Scoot's mother tells him that she knows Jerry is scared of her. "I'm just so goddamn lonely," she says.

This story told me enough about the turnaround of father-hate to make me a man of action, but still not a man of courage. So I insisted Mary Kay and Scoot come with me to my father's house. My plan was not to call him, like normal, but to skulk around in his bushes. It was a Friday night, usually a busy night for my father, and I thought that he might act a little differently around people who were not his son. Or even better, maybe I would see him off-duty, acting like all the other citizens of the world as we know it. Either way, I wanted to learn something new about him, about me. That was my plan. Mary Kay and Scoot both balked, so to Mary Kay I mentioned the sorry state of our marriage; to Scoot, his own father-problems.

"We all belong over there," I told them.

And they agreed, which finally brings us back to the place where Mary Kay, Scoot, and I are all hiding and waiting. It is around ten at night, and Mary Kay has just refused Scoot's racy key chain. Scoot is taking it pretty hard. First, he sniffles, coughs, and turns his face. Then he cries out loud and says *Oh god, I'm so sorry, oh my fucking god.* It turns out that I was right, that Scoot has come all this way from Germany to reunite with Mary Kay. He apologizes to me, says that I'm a pretty good egg, and that his sympathy for me was genuine. But Scoot says he can't help it. He goes on about how this is the do-or-die for he and Mary

Kay, about perspective and distance and second chances and all the choice phrases of love.

"I do love you," he says to Mary Kay. "How about it?"

"Please, please shut up," Mary Kay says.

"Thank you," I say.

"You shut up, too," Mary Kay says.

Then it's me who feels like crying, but Mary Kay's voice tells me that she's nowhere near tears herself, that she's reached the hard place that comes after crying. So me and Scoot both shut up. We drink the bourbon we brought with us and mutter about the cold wind. I'm about as low as a human being can go. I wonder if my father will ever come out of his house, and I get pretty morose, thinking that this is it, that I'll never have that good thing people call a "normal life." I feel like everything would be different, that I could be a decent man if I could just get some questions answered. Why, for example, do we find people like Scoot impressive because of his uniform, and people like my father pathetic because of his lack of one? What is it that makes a man take off his clothes on principle? What makes principle ugly to some and handsome to others? Does blood mean anything? Does history? What is it that lets one of us take comfort in another's misery? Do we ever know where the idea of the father leaves off and the true father kicks in? And where does that leave me?

Meanwhile, Scoot is grumbling and bitching under his breath this entire time. I'm trying to do some deep thinking about fathers and sons, and Scoot is asking if there are three bigger assholes in the entire world than the three of us. Mary Kay makes shushing sounds at him, but Scoot is obviously drunk and past caring. He gets louder, asking, "What the fuck do we think we're doing, sitting out here in the freezing cold?" and "What kind of morons are we?" and "I came all the way from Germany for this?" Mary Kay tells him to shut up with his dumb questions, and now they're both making a racket and I tell you, it is impossible for a man to *think* out here.

So I stand up. It is a gesture which in the movies comes before the drawing of pistols or the donning of tap shoes or some other expression of the confrontational male ego. I clear my throat, close my eyes, and in a voice loud enough to be heard all throughout my father's white-bread neighborhood on Top Notch Road, I ask: "Does anyone really want to know what's important in this world?"

"There he is," Mary Kay says, and hits me in the shin.

And there my father is, naked, shining, and holy-looking in the glow of the floodlight. Mary Kay and Scoot stand up with me, and we wait there quietly. Some of the neighbors must have heard us screeching and wailing, because they're out on their front stoops in their bathrobes. The neighbors have these baleful, searching expressions on their faces, and they're waiting, too. The wind has blown the clouds away and the sky is clear, the stars brilliant and beyond counting. My father still has his gray hair and his exposed, wrinkled body, but now he seems wise, patient, and fearless. I am hopeful. He looks at the three of us and then at his neighbors—their lawns dotted with ornamental windmills, pink flamingos, and lawn jockeys—and he smiles, and I think: This is what it was like when the world began, when the stars were all new and the mysteries unsolved, and all the ancient versions of our hardhearted selves stood around with their false idols, waiting to find out if they had ever asked any of the right questions.

Compensation

A few of us are worried about our friend Steve, a family man and trusted co-worker, who has just cut his right hand clean off with a table saw. Steve is supposed to use the table saw to make fiberglass shells, which is what he gets paid his seven dollars-an-hour for, not to cut off his right hand, for which he will not receive compensation. The shells themselves are eventually destined to become the nose cone of a space shuttle, or maybe the body of a canoe, or the roof of a tractor trailer. Old Steve has really done a number on his hand and on the normally unstoppable production process. We can all see Mr. Tolland, owner of Adirondack Fiberglass Co., talking on the cordless phone in his office and looking somewhat peeved and pacing. There is a sign out in front of the fiberglass plant which reads 173 ACCIDENT-FREE WORK DAYS. Tomorrow the sign will read *0*, which Mr. T. knows won't be exactly super for morale.

Those of us who are worried about Steve crowd around him as he sits on the floor, looking a little amazed and bleeding mightily. I mean, the blood is all over the place: on the concrete floor, on my shoes, and all over

89

Steve, obviously. Steve doesn't seem to mind the blood too much, maybe because he's in shock. But I am not in shock, and to be honest, I've got some deep anger over the blood and over Steve's extremely doubtful future. I've got the feeling that I might hit someone. This, I recently found out, is a political feeling. I'm considering a run for the position of union shop representative, and so I've been reading some of the union brochures and literature. I know that a woman named Emma Goldman once said: "The workers must meet violence with greater violence." I like her way of thinking, especially since it's pretty close to Steve's and my philosophy in high school. In those times, seven or so years ago, Steve and I did not yet have direct experience with occupational hazards or the marginal life of the working man. What we did have were memberships to the weight room at the YMCA, violent tendencies, sharp, non-book-learning minds, and a physical hostility to anyone in the Little Falls (NY) Jr.-Sr. High School who pretended that Steve and I were not impressive specimens of the Young American Male. Which no one did.

So I ask Steve if there is anyone in particular he would like me to hit.

"No thanks," Steve says. "You might want to get me a towel for my arm, though."

"Of course," I say, a little saddened that so much of time and power and secondary education is gone. "Done."

So I get Steve a towel and apply it to the stump of his right arm. But there still is this slight problem. I don't see Steve's hand anywhere. I ask if anyone knows where Steve's hand is, but no one does. Steve is understandably a little concerned, so I tell him not to worry, that someone has probably already taken care of it. Meanwhile, I see Mr. T. sneaking around the edges of the crowd, looking a little skittish. Seeing him doesn't give me a good feeling about Steve's hand. Last December, I left a nice pair of winter gloves down at the plant. They were not where I left them when I came in the next day. In fact, the gloves were sitting right on Mr. T.'s desk when I walked into his office to report them missing. *Those gloves cost me ten dollars,* I told him. *My property, my possession,* he said back. I know from my union reading that this behavior is not unusual, that Mr. T. and his kind are absolute pros at taking things that don't belong to them—things like time and money and human dignity. So why not a hand? is my theory. Of course, I don't share this line of thought with Steve. At least the towel and the pressure I'm putting on Steve's stump keeps him content for a while, until the paramedics come. When the paramedics finally get here, one of them is pushing people around, trying to get to Steve.

"Hey," I say. "Who do you think you are?"

"I'm only the guy who's here to save your life," he says.

"Not my life," I say, and point to Steve, who after all is the one on the floor, bleeding. Still, I am pretty glad to see the paramedic for Steve's sake, since, truth be told, I'm only the guy who sands the fiberglass shells and loads them in trucks back in the bay. Steve is the guy who does the measuring, calculating, visualizing, and cutting that makes the sanding and the loading possible. When he's finished, I have a go at the hardened shells, holding the sculpted fiberglass with one gloved hand while planing down the rough edges with an electric sander. There isn't going to be any more visualizing or cutting or sanding or anything today, especially since Steve's partner has been covered with Steve's blood and possibly even swallowed a little. He is busy in the bathroom, having a nervous fit, and I don't even feel a little sorry for him. I actually think Steve's partner is being pretty dramatic about swallowing some blood, especially with Steve sitting there on the floor with no hand. I ask you, is this solidarity? This is not solidarity. We all have our problems. Me, I've already reached my daily limit, itching-wise, because of all the fiberglass dust and flakes underneath my clothes, down my throat, and in my hair. When I get done sanding a load of shells, it looks like I've been through Christmas in Chernobyl, that is, if Russian Communists get to have Christmas, or if nuclear fallout looks like snow or fiberglass dust or anything. The union brochures don't really say anything about Russia.

Later on, I go visit Steve in the hospital. I have my jealousy over Steve's obvious professional superiority as a craftsman to my more manual labor, and I also have my jealousy over his beautiful wife, Loreen, and his two young daughters, Brittany and Shauna, who are potential beauty pageant material or at least department store kiddie models. Me, I do not have the beautiful things that Steve has: wife, daughters, new double-wide trailer, car that runs in bad weather, anything. Obviously, Steve is not jealous of me at all, which means he has a pure state of mind and being that I am also jealous of. To be true, Steve's and my friendship is pretty much in ruin over these jealousies, which I am ashamed of and helpless to arrest. But I am also terrified at the thought of his grieving, cute little girls, who are always in late-date Shirley Temple outfits and can dance and even sing a little at parties if coaxed. Plus, Steve has been my friend forever, and I am emotionally invested in his well-being.

Steve is awake when I get to the hospital. He's in the trauma ward and is pumped all full of drugs. There is some complication with his hand, as I find out. But Steve looks great and even glowing, maybe because of all the drugs and the trauma.

"Steve," I say. "You look absolutely wonderful."

"I do," he says.

"Just wonderful," I tell him.

"They can't find my hand," Steve says.

"Damn," I say. "I was worried about that."

"No one knows where it is. Not the doctors or anyone down at the plant. I wonder if you could try and find it for me."

"Definitely," I say, a little touched by the request. "Don't even worry about it."

Then I sit there and watch Steve heal by small degrees while I figure the odds of me ever recovering his hand. As I said, things have gone differently for me and Steve since high school. That is life. For instance, I like to say that Steve is the kind of guy who buys his large appliances down at Sears on EZ-credit, while I'm the kind of guy who goes out to Curboy's junkyard and shoots at old washers and dryers with an air rifle. But this makes we wonder if I am also the kind of guy who can actually find someone's missing hand. In fact, I sit watching Steve for so long and in such a hole of silence that Steve, too, probably questions the wisdom of asking me to undertake such an important, life-changing task; probably forgets why or if we were ever friends in the first place;

probably forgets that he ever even had a right hand; probably forgets that his whole, moderately happy life has now been reduced to one work-related accident. What Steve definitely does forget is to stay awake, his black hair growing damp with the fatigue and the pain as I sit there, slowly and terribly disappointing him while he sleeps.

Finally, Steve's wife comes into the room and I get up to go. They don't give us health insurance down at work, but Steve has his insurance through Loreen, who is the attendance secretary at the Monroe Street Elementary School. So, another reason for more jealousy and less friendship. Of course, it's pretty expensive having a family, and it's especially expensive having two daughters as beautiful as Steve's. The hospital is probably the one place where Steve can afford to go.

"Where are you going?" Loreen asks me as I am leaving.

"I'm going to find Steve's hand," I tell her.

"I don't doubt it," she says doubtfully, perfect tears welling up in each eye the way tears should when your husband's body parts and maybe your whole future are in the hands of someone like me.

After I get home from the hospital, I stay up all night, drinking coffee, and stomping around my apartment. I think about Steve in the hospital bed and Loreen's tears and Steve's missing hand and their pretty sorry prospects for future happiness. I think about my own sorry prospects, living in a mill town of five thousand in upstate New York where there isn't even a mill any more, just a fiberglass plant where your lack of skills can get you six dollars-an-hour and a fairly pessimistic view of the human condition. I think about my apartment itself, an efficiency over Ponzo's Pizzeria with no working lock on the front door and nothing behind the door to steal except for the smells coming up from Ponzo's, which aren't bad.

Finally, I think: Enough.

By the time I get to work in the morning, I am promising myself that the shit stops here, that I will not disappoint Steve and his family, that I will no longer feel this helpless about life. I am so optimistic about recovering Steve's hand that I bring a little Igloo beer cooler with me, full of ice, so I can rush the hand to the hospital and not do any more damage that Steve and the hand cannot afford. I tell some of the others about Steve's situation, which raises the level a couple notches on the outrage meter. I say that I'm pretty sure I know who has Steve's hand. Steve's missing hand is part of a pattern, I tell them. I point to Mr. T.'s glassed-in office and his nice mini-refrigerator, where he keeps sandwiches and beer and things. Do we have a mini-refrigerator in the break room? I ask. Do we have an antique wood desk with drawers that lock or a four-foot-high filing cabinet or a portable phone? Do we have health insurance? Do we have vacation time, with pay? Do we have Steve's hand? The others see the wisdom in this kind of thinking and are yelling and their mood is ugly. I mention Emma Goldman. Some volume on the yelling is lost, but not much.

Not to be crude, but it looks like I have a lock on that union-rep position.

So a bunch of us decide to storm into Mr. T.'s office to demand satisfaction. Mr. T. is behind his desk, sweating out a visit from a trio of OSHA officials. The OSHA officials are all wearing surgical masks, which we are allowed and actually required by law to also wear.

One of the officials turns and sees us come in, and asks: "Where are all your masks?"

"Where is Steve Yerina's right hand?" I ask him.

The three OSHAS then lean over Mr. T.'s desk in conference. They are all whispering and taking notes, which I read as a sign of progress. As the OSHAS talk, their breath makes small, quick impressions on the surface of the white surgical masks in the manner of a child's fist punching the inside of a hot air balloon, not in the manner of genuine human communication.

After a few minutes of this, Mr. T. stands straight up. He has a nervous, almost queasy look on his face. "Why don't you all take the rest of the day off, with pay," he says.

The majority of the others decide that the offer does in fact give them some satisfaction. I plead with them to reconsider, to think about Steve and Steve's family and so on. But even I recognize that some passion is missing in the pleading. To be honest, I am pretty tired, maybe because I was up all night worrying about Steve. To be even more honest, I wouldn't mind taking the rest of the day off with pay myself, even though Steve is counting on me and I swore that the shit would stop here and I know my guilt will be unbearable later on. But still.

So we take the rest of the day off.

I remember once, about seven years ago, when Steve and I spent an entire Sunday night in Gill McKenney's cornfield. We had two long-handled clippers and an abundance of trash bags, and with an absolute harmony of motion and purpose we cut a giant, perfectly round circle into that field, leaving a small, solid O of corn in the middle of the circle. Then we put the cut corn into the trash bags, loaded the bags into the back of Steve's pickup, and drove out to the Mohawk River, where we weighed the bags of corn down with rocks and dumped them.

The next morning, our high school, which was right next to Gill McKenney's cornfield, was up in arms over this mysterious circle in the dead center of a pretty ordinary cornfield. The entire school assumed the circle was the product of some higher, extra-intelligent power, and took the morning off to visit the site. The photography students brought their cameras, the studio art students their sketch pads. The Catholic students, who were supposed to be on released-time for religious training, prayed violently. Even the janitors, who were at the school all the time, at night and on weekends, left the building.

Steve and I were seniors then and in perfect control of our world and each other. When everyone was out at the cornfield, Steve and I snuck back to the school and burned it all the way to the ground. We were so sick of them making us take all those classes when we could be out there, say, at the fiberglass plant, making our money. Which we did.

Well, I think, that was a genius piece of diversion. It probably won't take that much this time, which is good as I'll be by myself. I'll probably only need a car fire, a nice car fire in the parking lot with the shadow figures of the other workers and foremen and Mr. T. jumping and diving in the flames while I'm inside, searching for Steve's right hand. Mr. T. probably has it locked in his file cabinet or desk drawer or maybe, if he has a conscience, hidden in his mini-refrigerator. Wherever it is, I'll find the hand and bring it to Steve. After all, I gave him my word.

A Cabin
on a Lake

Every year, I, Cynthia Marie Furlong, shake off the ball and chain
of this predictable old world and run up north to Caroga Lake,
where the snowmobile races are our Kentucky Derby and where the
summer carnival features palomino carousel horses made by Seminole
Indians during the Cold War. The horses are deformed and near-
unridable from exposure and normal northern wear-and-tear. But then
again, those Indians couldn't know how drifting snow causes wooden
palominos to warp and mange, and I don't know how those Indians felt
about making wooden facsimiles of real palominos, and so I won't lay
blame or make assumptions about cultural differences and the weather.

Last summer, I saw Juice—just one in a trio of bad loves I'm here to
tell you about—up there at Caroga Lake working as a carny and taking
tickets for the carousel. I recognized Juice from his high local celebrity
as the varsity football coach for the Ilion Golden Bombers, which was
why I was surprised to find him balancing a little delicately on a stool,
taking people's stubs and stuffing them in a burlap pouch that said

Sherman Williams. I stepped up, handed him my ticket and said, "Coach Juice Myers."

"Was," he said, without apparent shame. "I was just fired. I was unable to teach my men the philosophy of the wishbone offense."

His honesty made me brave and greedy for even more of that good honesty. So I said: "Rumor says you were taken with drinking chilled red wine in your office at school."

"That too," he said.

"And that you had a weakness for senior cheerleaders with scholarship potential."

"Not that," he said and I believed him. I climbed up on my warped wooden steed and rode it around and around, which is a position most so-called intellectuals would not be caught in and where I do my very best thinking. When I dismounted, Juice and I got married. For two months we lived in a rent-free company cabin on the lake, with thick screens in the windows and blue curtains with daisies flapping in the wind. Outside, the black flies were grouped in divisions like Roman soldiers. Inside, we would sit on the Hide-a-Bed and drink Juice's red wine, and Juice would tell me all the details of his working life. Juice felt that when you took a job you became a part of the job's history. He's the one who explained to me the history of the carousel horses and the Seminole Indians who made them. Juice would also spend hours talking about football legend and lore: about the Galloping Ghost Red Grange, and the legalization of the forward pass, and the rise and fall of Woody Hayes, that sweet, violent genius who was the pride of Ohio State University and the rest of the world of men. Juice would get a little teary, thinking about this world from which he was now estranged, and he would drink too much red wine and ask: "Do you love me? Are we actually in love already?" These are exactly the questions you do not expect to come out of the mouth of a big bubba ex-football coach with a mild drinking problem and seasonal carnival employment, and you should answer them with great enthusiasm and with no mind toward the institutions of permanency and full-time employment.

But as usually happens in this brand of story, the summer ended two months later, by which I mean the carnival shut down and the carousel ceased its revolution. Juice became visibly distressed. He quit eating. He halved his push-up regimen. All of Juice's big-man charm and quiet self-possession left him.

One day I found Juice sitting in the kitchen, fingering the straps of his ticket apron. "I don't think I can go back to civilization," he told me.

"We're not going back to civilization," I said. "We're going back home."

"And what exactly am I going to do there?" Juice asked. "What is a shamed football coach supposed to do?"

I sat down and gave the situation real thought. I suggested janitorial work, a circulation desk job at the county library, and enrollment in a continuing-ed program. These weren't just the options available for tainted ex-sports heroes. These were the options. Juice shook his head at each suggestion. Not to be obvious, but I sensed real disaster.

"Well," I told him, "You don't have to do anything at all." I said this without sarcasm or ulterior motive, but Juice looked at me as if I were a creature from an entirely different physical and moral planet.

But he had no other ideas. So we returned to Little Falls. I went back to my waitressing job and to my boss, Jim, who was another one of my terrible romances. In fact, I had been married to Jim for three whole months two years earlier, and he hadn't completely gotten over it yet.

"You've missed two months' work," he said.

"Jim! Look at me. I am married," I said, and then told him the whole story. I gushed and so on. Jim shook his head the entire way through my description of Juice.

"I don't like it," he said. "I can tell already, that boy Juice just can't settle down." This is exactly what a man with a degree in hotel management, a fifty-two-inch chest, and a two-year subscription to *Reader's Digest* will say when you tell him a story about love.

I worked six hours that same night, and came home with thirty-two dollars in tips. When I got home, Juice was lying on the floor with his size eleven Nikes resting on the couch. He said he couldn't bring himself to do one sit-up. Not one push-up either. This was serious. You've never seen a man so concerned with the well-being of his stomach muscles as my Juice. His belly looked more like a waffle than it did any part of normal human anatomy.

"I love you, Juice," I said immediately. "I made sixty-four dollars tonight."

Juice looked up at me with the blossoming resignation of a man who has lost the will to take part in life's to-and-fro. He said: "Our love can't last, you probably know that."

I pretended not to hear his prediction. Juice said it again and I denied his claim repeatedly, even though what he said was the absolute truth.

At the age of twenty-two, four years before I met Juice, I gave myself a good hard look and discovered I was still a girl at that late date and dying a slow death in my hometown. This was 1988, and Little Falls itself was also dying, with the paper mills leaving for Mississippi, or turning themselves into cosmetics wholesalers or custom-made furniture workshops run by late-blooming hippies. The hippies were the happiest folks around, what with their appreciation of the sublime and their generous trust funds. I had just graduated with honors from the community college, which sometimes hired the hippies to teach studio art classes and, in a pinch, political science.

Having realized I was dying, I had a conversation with my father, who had just been laid off. My father worked at the paper mill for thirty-one years, a tenure he found one year too many for drama, four years too few for full retirement.

"Dad, I'm in agony," I said. "Let's talk about my life."

"Agreed," he said. "I am in agony, too."

"Dad, please."

"Cindy," he said, "I worked at that mill for thirty-one years. What kind of man am I now? It's got so bad, I've started wearing bathrobes day and night."

This was true. My father was wearing a sea-green bathrobe with his initials on the chest pocket. I had given him the robe for his birthday. It was soft.

"Dad, please," I told him. "You called in sick every bank holiday. Sweeping the pulp and the dust gave you a cough and turned your pee all green."

"You get used to it," he said. "I didn't even think about wearing a bathrobe when I was working. Now I'm special-ordering them through catalogs."

That's when I knew that my father was dying, too. I loved him too much to do anything but think about myself. I was back at my old high school, substitute teaching ninth-grade English and study halls. You can't actually be expected to teach study hall, so I sat and listened to the debate rage on between Ford and Chevy owners, except these were fourteen-year-old kids who didn't own Fords or Chevys or anything. Me, I owned a Ford but had absolutely no opinions on the matter.

If you are at this kind of moment in the sorry old world, you have few choices:

You can join a church: Catholic if possible, Baptist if necessary.

You can develop a drinking problem. This you might already be working on.

You can keep living with your parents. The three of you will develop what your mother calls "space issues." Your father will talk about putting an addition on the house. He will call it "the apartment." He will go so far as to purchase a self-help manual for carpenters, and dog-ear the section entitled: "Emergency Plans for Unexpected Guests."

You can begin hating your parents, with an eye toward their diminishing life expectations and the great beyond.

You can do all of the above, not well, but often and maybe forever.

Or you can get up and walk out of that study hall, throw off the expectations of gender, region, and class, and do something unlikely and by Jesus a little brilliant.

This I did. I lit out for Richmond, Virginia, where I became a tire saleswoman. The world needs its citizens well-versed in the effects of front wheel drive on all-weather radials. No one ever thought I'd become a tire saleswoman, which is why I became one. And I was good at it.

I liked Richmond all right, with its fine manners, low expectations, hot brick and weather. I lived on the second floor of a noble, run-down brownstone and found plenty of people interested in the life of a tire saleswoman from upstate New York. I went to parties where they served expensive liquor, where I sweated mightily, and where the male playwrights, prep school teachers, and playboys with soft positions in commerce committed vicious libel against homosexuals. When they got drunk enough and had disgusted their dates and wives into abandonment or irreversible punch-drinking, these boys admitted they would and did make pretty good stereotypical homosexuals themselves, what with their accents and good clothes and wilting self-confidence. Then they asked me if it were true that all northerners hated the South.

"Is this really the South?" I asked them.

"Yes," they said. "Do you hate us?"

"Yes," I said.

This made them so happy.

At one of these parties I met a man with muscular arms, young features, and a finely wrinkled face. I myself am average pretty and have an honest face that inspires confidence in men. This man and I had a drink together, which then grew into seven drinks. Three hours later, around two in the morning, he confessed to me that he had never reached puberty. This is the kind of thing men tend to say after seven drinks and so it didn't faze me much.

"Why haven't you reached puberty?" I asked him.

"Why do you think?"

"Fear," I guessed. "Lack of interest."

"That is incorrect," he told me. "Both times. I am interested and unafraid. I also have a condition. My voice stays high. My features are permanently young. My skin gets older from exposure."

He said this without sorrow and with a dignity that I found extraordinarily beautiful. He was a jazz singer. I believed him when he said he was fearless. His young, quivering voice was ironic but hopeful. Everyone knew about his condition from a sensational article in the local entertainment weekly. When he sang "Begin the Beguine" at the

Paradise in his painful, trembling soprano, all the old men and women wept and promised out loud to stop ruining their lives in the pursuit of other people's greatness.

As you will have guessed, this man was my first love chronologically, the third in this story of awful loves. His name was Robert.

For several months straight we stayed at his apartment and played board games and were in love. Robert's condition did not make love impossible, but only required a little extra imagination and determination. I am happy to say that I had both, as did Robert. Robert also had the sense that he should be doing something of great importance with his life. He wrote me long love letters promising to do this and this and that. Then he would send me letters through the mail, which he said made the contents official. Once the letters arrived, we'd lie in bed and Robert would read them out loud and dramatically, as if reciting Shakespeare or Homer or some other expert on love and ambition. He would unbutton my Firestone Tire Palace shirt with one hand and with the other gesture wildly while he talked about his desire for the improbable. Robert said singing was fine and good, but that he longed to write history books full of interesting facts and controversial conclusions. He said this was all possible without the aid of a graduate education or an informed sense of audience. I was impressed, and counted my blessings daily. How often can a girl leave home and shuck her expected life and do something absolutely unusual for her daily bread? And in doing so, how often does that same girl meet someone equally determined and not at all tragic, and love that person not for the way he fits into her grand scheme but because of love? How often?

The tricky thing about throwing off your expectations, however, is that you are expected to accept new ones by default. These expectations find you without you even knowing it. Soon, I started having these kinds of conversations at the Firestone Tire Palace down there in Richmond:

Me, to a customer: "You don't just need an alignment. You don't just need new tires, either. What you've got is a tire rod problem. You need a new tire rod in the front."

The customer, male: "Say that again. Your fine diagnosis."

Me, disgusted and antagonistic: "Rod. You're in need of a new rod."
Him, titillated: *"Really."*

When the sale of automobile parts becomes embroiled in the world of desire and fetish, and when all lubrication policies become one-in-the-same, you have reached an impasse that cannot be solved by negotiation, compromise, or even bloodletting. The only resolution is to flee. This I did.

"Robert," I said, "I am in need of greener pastures. I'm throwing off my expectations again."

"Wonderful," he said. "I'm throwing off my expectations, too."

"What exactly do people expect of you?" I asked.

This question wounded Robert deeply and for reasons I couldn't then imagine.

We decided to move to North Carolina, where I rejected my recent expectations by accepting my original ones. I did exactly what a woman with some education and limited life-experience will do in times of crisis, and began waiting tables at the Whale Bone Cafe at Milepost 11, in Kitty Hawk. Robert buried himself in the local history scene. He found the Outer Banks tragic and self-deceiving, and kept firing off inquiring letters to historical societies and DAR cadres. Robert had a nose for neglected evidence. He could sweet talk a spinster archivist in a second. He told one old lady from Nag's Head on the phone: "I'm writing a book about you."

"That's lovely," she said. Her name was Elizabeth and she bequeathed small grants to projects with local significance. Robert promised to include her name in the acknowledgments, and she gave him seventy-five dollars and a Roanoke Lost Colony key chain.

Robert worked on the introduction to that book for three months. When he finished he asked me to look it over. I had just worked eight hours at the restaurant, had tartar sauce smeared all over my official Whale Bone Cafe T-shirt and might not have been in the mood for history and proofreading.

I still have that introduction.

The legend of the name of Nag's Head, North Carolina goes like this. During the time when people still used horses, the citizens of the town tied lanterns to their horses' necks at nights. These were broken horses and young, healthy ones. Ponies with pure bloodlines and mules, donkeys, servant animals. The people of this part of Bodie Island (before it was called that) didn't care about the bloodlines or temperament or anything. They only cared about those lanterns. Quality for this nighttime job was not an issue. The horses couldn't outlive their usefulness unless they outlived living. It was the fairest system around.

At night, the horses and the lights and their invisible masters walked along the dunes, within eyesight of the Atlantic. They were above and beyond the shore, not on it. You couldn't tell this from the ocean. When the horses walked and lights rose and fell it was like the stern lights of anchored boats, bobbing in the ocean swells. At night, those island Tar Heels would bring out ten, twelve horses and set them walking on the dunes. Distance is a weird concept at night, from sea. There is the rocking imbalance to contend with, the tricky inner ear, the conspiracy between current and wind, the crank moon. There are potential mutinies of all kinds. But the most important factor in sailing and landing a boat is knowledge of the land and its long arms: its sandbars, reefs, sharp rocks. Its concealed weapons. When a sailor at night sees the rise and fall of lights, ten at a time, he thinks of safe harbor. He thinks if he can reach those lights he will be safe from the grind of rock and sand on wooden hull.

There is no way of telling what the sailor thinks when he finally runs aground. Maybe somebody has led off the horses and their lights by then, preserving the secret of the trick for those who profit from it. There is no fair play in dry-land piracy. The sailor may not even know what is happening when his hurt ship is overrun by these smart country people and their weapons; when they go into the hold and take what they need, what they might use, and drown the rest. Even when he is about to die, he still may have no idea. He is still wondering about the certainty of those bobbing lights, about how he has completely misread his life, how he has believed too deeply in the constants of landing.

Enough. There is more about the Lost Colony at Roanoke, Blackbeard, the Wright Brothers, and the continuum of modern tourism, but you get the idea. I know a little bit about scholarly objectivity and grammar. When I finished reading his introduction I turned to Robert, and told him the truth. I was too tired for spin control or feelings or even the lover's famous tact.

"It is dramatic but without quotes," I told him. "It's also a little informal. Choppy, too."

Robert was stunned. "Anything else?" he asked.

I paused in consideration and then said: "You might be some kind of Marxist."

This set Robert off, for reasons that might have eluded Marx himself. First he stared at me. Then he made aspersions against my intelligence and slavery to convention. Then Robert started in drinking and never stopped. I rarely saw him. He stopped coming back to our two-room apartment in Kill Devil Hills. One day in October he finally came into the restaurant. It was four in the afternoon, and there was no one there but myself and the raw bar manager, a forty-year-old ex-professional surfer named Sören. We were pitching dimes against the wall when Robert blazed in.

"I know you were right," he said to me. "I admit it. I don't care about history at all. I don't much care about success, either. What I do care about is other people thinking me a failure."

"Wow," Sören said.

"I understand," I told Robert.

This made Robert hate me even more.

But I did understand. I understood two weeks later when Robert kidnapped me in the restaurant parking lot. I did nothing to resist, acting like a woman would in the movies or the Bible or in the homes of recent immigrants. Robert drove to a secluded spot near the Wright Brothers Memorial. The wind was up and the dunes were shifting mysteriously in the dark. Robert turned on the inside car light and had me read his old love letters aloud. They were still beautiful. In one letter he even wrote me his age, which he refused to tell anyone else. But I won't tell it to you. It doesn't mean anything.

There was one more thing: in each letter he promised me that he wouldn't be a singer forever.

"And why not a singer?" I asked him. "What was wrong with singing?"

"I had a beautiful voice," he said. "I was good."

"Yes," I said. "Yes, yes, yes."

"But everyone loved my singing because I was a freak. It was expected. It was automatic. I was a better singer because I was a freak."

"That's not true," I said.

"And you loved me because I was a freak. I expected that, too."

"Not true, either."

"But the truth is I wanted to be known as someone who could do something unexpected."

I had left home fearing home itself meant the slow destruction of my sense of family, future, and self-worth. I thought my departure from the dying economy, cold winters, and depressing predictability of upstate New York was success of a kind. But I watched Robert walk away through the sand, my heart dying right there in his shrinking tracks, and realized that we are always destroying ourselves with an eye toward someone else's regard, regardless of geography. I had thrown off my expectations, approached contentment, and watched my first love give himself an ego and then give away happiness. Well, I thought. Time to go home.

It was 1989 now and my parents were already elderly. My father had given up on the mill hiring him back, and had started working part-time delivery for the local auto-parts store. There was no talk of my mother getting a job. There was no talk of my father's job except that he had one. There was no more talk of building an addition on the house. There was barely any talk at all, except when my parents talked about how happy they were to see me. They talked about it so much that I finally moved into my own apartment. The apartment had once been the initiation room at the old Masonic Temple. At night I could barely sleep because of all the ghosts of lost power and white magic and political mystery washing over me. Next door, a woman and her three young children had taken up residence in the old game room. The woman promised to kill the children nightly for all the noise they made and the years they were stripping off her life. Those kids did make some impressive, animalistic sounds. I think it was the ghosts that made them so bad.

I started working for Jim right away at his place, Jim's Lonely Pines Restaurant. I remembered Jim from high school—two classes ahead of me—with his impressive cleft chin and easy disposition. I also remembered Jim as perpetually upbeat and aphoristic, qualities that he carried into adulthood and the work place. Jim supplied us waitresses and bus boys with a saying-a-day on the bulletin board in the break room. He offered up pearls of wisdom on the disposable placemats. The place itself was really a diner, but Jim called it a restaurant. It didn't matter. The corned beef hash was something special. People would have come to the diner no matter what Jim called it.

"It doesn't matter what the place is called," Jim said to me. "A rose is a rose."

"What?" I asked him.

"Same shit, different day," he said.

"What?" I asked. "What are you saying?"

But despite our problems in basic communication, I began to think of Jim in ways beyond our formal employer-employee relationship. Jim had a job and no apparent anxiety. He made people feel comfortable, and he made me feel comfortable to the point of absolute confusion and medium physical attraction. I felt the need to take hold of my life, and so I decided to start asking the questions that might lead me toward happiness. One day, nine months after starting work at the Lonely Pines, I barged into Jim's office and said, "Name your ambitions."

"What?" he asked me.

"Are you dissatisfied with your life?"

"No. Happy as a pig."

"Do you want something more than this? Are you afraid you'll never be anything but a restaurant owner?"

Jim smiled. "I am not afraid," he said. He then kissed me full-on and without warning, just like they do in the movies. It wasn't the smoothest thing in the world, but it was dramatic. In the real world, drama and passion aren't necessarily the same thing, and sometimes you have to settle.

When we paused in our mashing some time later, Jim asked me if I would like to marry him.

"You're a nice man. But I might not be in love with you."

"Don't sweat the details," he said.

"Then let's do it," I said.

"Super," he said.

Three months later I left him because he said, "The proof is in the pudding" every day for the entire month of January. I wouldn't explain to Jim why I was leaving, because his sayings gave him such happiness. The mystery left Jim with some bitterness. Still, he let me work at the restaurant out of fairness, which makes it easier to understand why he offered Juice a job—at my request—two years, one divorce, and one remarriage later.

"I've got a big heart," Jim told me.

"Yes," I said, and relayed the message to Juice. This was now after Thanksgiving. Juice had been sitting on the couch all fall. Our love had begun to wear thin in unimagined places. Like Robert, Juice didn't mind being a failure, but he was paralyzed at the idea of people believing him one. This transformed our marriage and my apartment into a major state of asylum. Juice hadn't looked for a job. He hadn't complained about his unemployment. He hadn't romanticized other people's employment. He hadn't developed an interest in politics nor had he renewed his interest in sports. He wasn't interested in intellectual self-improvement or the TV. He wasn't interested in stating or proving his love to me in new and inventive ways. He had even lost interest in looking and acting like the big man that he was. Even the intensity of his drinking hadn't increased, which is rumored to happen with people who lose interest in everything else. The upshot was that Juice hadn't done anything at all. I began to forget why I had loved Juice in the first place. I had no friends to confide in: they were all busy having the same problems, or were too happy that they weren't having the same problems to be interested in mine. So I gave

myself advice, and asked Jim to give Juice a job at the restaurant, washing
dishes and busing tables.

"Thank Jim for me," Juice said. "I don't want the job."

"Juice, the world has completely lost its damn head," I said. "This
is the job. You want this job."

It was snowing outside and was starting to look like a different
world. It was pretty. I felt this change coming on and it felt good and
right the way changes sometimes do. When it became clear that Juice
didn't feel the same thing, I started crying. Juice pretty much fell to
pieces, thinking that he had driven me to such a mournful state. It was
a convincing performance on my part. He said he'd take the job if I
would just stop crying. So I stopped crying. I don't feel even a damn bit
guilty about it and neither would you.

But before Jim had Juice start working, he stretched out his big
heart some more and gave us a weekend off.

"Why don't you use my cabin this weekend?" he said to me. One
month after our divorce, Jim had bought a vacation place up in the
Adirondacks. He said it was a present to himself.

"Are you sure?" I asked him.

"Come on," he said. "It's on the lake. It's got a fireplace. Just ask and
it's yours. Don't even bother asking. It's yours anyways. I haven't been
up there since the summer. It may be dirty. I apologize in advance."

"But why, Jim?" I asked, sensing some kind of guile.

"Because I want you kids to have a running start."

"A fighting chance," I said.

"Absotutely," he said. "Whichever."

So Juice and I lit out for Jim's cabin for the weekend. Jim said his
cabin was on Lake Pleasant, thirty miles north of Caroga Lake. The
further we drove, the more our present reality parted and rearranged
like the snow itself as we drove through it. Our life once again took on
the happy limits of flight. Juice thought he could see some hope in his
new job now that it was behind him. He thought he could see hope
period. He grew in posture and stature. I fell in love again as I read the
directions to Jim's place out loud while Juice drove.

To get to Jim's place, drive north for an hour, into Speculator. Turn left onto Alpine Drive, past the Speculator Firehouse, but before the Pine Valley public golf course. Then take the next right, an unmarked dirt road with Vic's Live Bait and Boat Rental on the corner. The road will fork after about fifty feet, so veer right like dependable Jim tells you to. You'll see rows and rows of trailers, but no lake. You might think you have taken a wrong turn, but you have not. Be patient, because you're very nearly there.

Drive a half mile further: you'll find Jim's cabin on the right and you'll also find that Jim's cabin isn't really a cabin, and it isn't on Lake Pleasant either. Jim's cabin is actually a metal trailer: white on the top, blue on the bottom, with stencil half-moon designs as the top border. To the left, looking at it from the road, there is a woodpile and next to the wood pile a picnic table, half-buried in snow and heavy with exposure. Further back from the road, there is a tin storage shed with the roof half caved-in; the double-doors are held together by a padlock with the key in it. The whole property is surrounded by spruce and pine, all young like you, not thick or tall enough yet to hide the trailers neighboring Jim's place on either side. On the west side of the trailer is a wooden deck. Climb the stairs to the deck and look out, Columbuslike, as if seeing a new world. You should see more trailers and trees and then nothing but air. That will be the lake.

"Well," one of you should say.

"Yes," the other should say back.

But when you are in love or want to be, and are fighting the collusion of circumstance, inflated expectations, and a vision of nature influenced by old Henry David Thoreau and not United Steel and the limited finances of the rural working class, do the following: retreat to your car, turn the heat on high and reassess your priorities. Say to yourselves: Do we need some kind of mansion? Say: We do not need some kind of mansion. Say: We do need each other, of course. Then, get out of the car, resume the honeymoon, knock the snow off your boots, and unlock the door to the cabin.

But once you find that the key you have is not the key to Jim's trailer, then you are absolutely on your own, and no amount of good feeling or high principle or class consciousness will save you.

I assured Juice that the key was the right one, even after I felt and knew that Jim had given us the wrong key. *That he had given us the wrong goddamn key.* There were two outside locks and we tried both of them. But the only thing that key was good for was marking up the trailer, which I did, carving a half-inch deep scratch from one end of the trailer to the other. I put a good sweat into it. By the time I finished, Juice was gone. I stood there defeated and watched his footprints trail off into the snow just like Robert's into the sand, the only real difference being a little weather, a little more desperation, and a little less time.

Does it need saying, I moved back in with Jim once I got back to Little Falls and started thinking about some reasonable kind of future. After all, there were the laws of probability, stability, and relative happiness to consider. Jim was still dependable, and for some reason, still interested in my female companionship. I told Jim that I still didn't think I loved him; but I also admitted that my history with Robert and Juice suggested that love didn't mean much anyway. Right on, Jim said. He pointed out that, unlike Robert and Juice, he loved his job and remained absolutely unconcerned about losing it or finding another one. Jim also said he was relationship-minded and success-oriented; he encouraged me to quit my waitressing job, and try to get a leg up at the high school. This I did. The kids were good to me but the faculty were absolute Huns. They knew all about my personal history and had no pity. Those teachers can really get their hooks into you, what with their immense reserves of professional bitterness and know how. But still, once the school year ended, I had hope that I would eventually wear them down, and they'd let me in on their secrets of lesson planning and early retirement.

As for Juice, I heard nothing about him for nearly eight months. Then, last week, Jim told me someone had spotted him up on Route 29, running a souvenir shack, and selling wooden figurine Indians. I took the news as some kind of closure.

"Jim," I said, remembering Juice's history lesson about the carousel up at Caroga Lake, "this story begins and ends with Indians. I know that the story of Juice and me is over because of the Indians he's selling."

Jim claimed this was all wrong. "People hear what they want to hear," he told me. Jim said that the Indians didn't stand for anything I didn't know already. "It was you who decided it was over," he said. "It was all you," and I let myself agree with him.

These days, Jim and I lie in bed after work and I listen to him talk. When we are fully stretched out, my ear comes right up to his voice box. In that position I can hear and feel the hum of Jim's throat as he tells me the ways in which he and I are different from Juice and Robert, my true, bad loves. I am honest with Jim and tell him that I still think of them, out in the world without me, especially Juice who is so close by in body and in memory. Jim says he understands, but he also insists that the past is the past.

"Trust me on this one," he says. "You and me, we're the real thing."

So finally, this is me: I, twenty-seven-year-old Cynthia Marie Furlong, have a potential career, a good, dependable man for a life-partner, and a secure place in the world. This is what we all want, is it not? So why then do I still feel so unsatisfied? Maybe it's because I still have so many unanswered questions. For instance, for all Jim's solid predictability and reliability and for all his talk, why won't he tell me what our real thing is? What is the real thing? Does the real thing actually exist? Maybe we should expect to settle for something less than the real thing. Maybe we should expect less from life, and from love. But what is love? Maybe this is the problem: that I still dream that real love is out there and that it will rise above the daily needs and details of this rotten world. I still dream that one night I will shake off my uncertainty, rudely interrupt Jim's speech-making, and say: "You know Jim, you say lots of things. And sometimes you're right, and sometimes you are not." What if this shocks Jim into an instant and long-overdue hatred? What if he wants to wash his hands of our personal history and send me off with an immediate, emotionally cathartic, and financially liberating alimony settlement? In my dream this is exactly what happens. In my dream I get up out of our king-sized bed, run to my car, and find Juice just where Jim said I would, sitting on the side of Route 29, hawking wooden Indians sculpted in positions of sitting, paddling, scalping. I kiss Juice; he kisses me. We drive up to Jim's place and I take Jim's ax from the storage shed, break down the door to his trailer, and Juice and I live in there forever, undisturbed, in perfect happiness. If Jim knew of this dream, he'd say: Cindy, you're fooling yourself. But am I not fooling myself now? What is the difference between the dream and the reality? And if there is no difference, then why is it taking me so long to reject the reality once and for all and follow the dream? In this dream, sitting in Jim's trailer with Juice, I ask myself this exact question: Cindy, why has it taken you so long? Because if all happiness costs you is one good Stanley ax, the destruction of a metal door, someone else's fleeting pain, and a healthy amount of self-deception, and what you get back is a nice cabin on a lake, an unlikely lover, and a future filled with no expectations and an abundance of good, cheap red wine, then what exactly is the harm in that?

Plowing
the
Secondaries

My brother and I are out plowing the secondaries the morning after a big spring snowstorm—my brother in one plow, me behind him in another—and I can see my brother is going way too fast, and I think: If he doesn't watch out he is going to hit something. And then he does not watch out and does hit something. It is a woman. My brother keeps going after he hits her, big flumes of snow curling and fanning out to the sides of the plow, as he barrels down Paines Hollow Road on the way to hitting something else. In the eight years he's been plowing, my brother has hit cows, parked cars, telephone poles, mailboxes, even other plows. Usually, I don't even bother getting out of my plow to see the thing he's hit. Usually, I just get him on the CB and say: "You dumb son of a bitch, you just hit another Holstein," etc. Then we finish plowing and I hope he doesn't hit anything else and ruin the plow blade, because it's my snow-removal business and my brother has ruined plenty of blades already, and believe me the blades are worth much more than my brother.

But this is the first time he's hit a human being. So I stop, get out of my plow, and go look for the woman. I find her twenty feet into the field next to the road. She is beautiful, lying there face up on a foot of wind-whipped newly fallen snow, her long black hair spread out fanlike beneath her, her checks apple-red from the cold. The woman doesn't look dead at all, no blood anywhere that I can see, nothing severed or disfigured. I lean over her, put my ear to her heart. I don't hear any heartbeat, but then again I have my hat pulled down over my ears and she has on a heavy down jacket and the plow is idling and rattling loudly behind me.

So I take off my hat, unzip her jacket, and lean over again to get a more definitive read on her heartbeat, because suddenly I *need* to know whether she is dead or alive. The woman is just so beautiful—lying there peacefully, watching me with these perfectly round, perfectly blue unblinking eyes—that I think I might actually be falling in love with her, just like that, and if so I *need* to know whether she is dead or alive, because that will change the way I approach the situation, obviously.

But then, leaning over her the way I am, I get this bad memory of last Friday night. Last Friday night, I was out late at the Renaissance, talking with my sister-in-law, who also has black hair and rosy cheeks and who also is beautiful. My sister-in-law was wearing this scooped-neck sweater that exposed her white, jutting collarbone, which in the light of the bar was a brilliant, precious thing, something less like an actual collarbone and more like a *whalebone* in its brilliance and its preciousness. While my sister-in-law was telling me a story about her job—she works as a bank teller—I was thinking: You cannot stand there and just *look* at a whalebone, man, a whalebone is a thing that needs to be *cherished.* So right in the middle of my sister-in-law's story about next-day-deposit-this and roll-of-quarters-that, I leaned over and kissed her exposed collarbone.

I saw immediately that my sister-in-law had not taken my kissing her collarbone in the spirit in which it was intended. Her face got flaming red, and she tightened her hands into tiny fists and started beating them against the sides of her legs.

"What in the hell do you think you're doing?" she asked.

"Relax," I said. "You should feel honored."

"What are you talking about?"

And because I was desperate to communicate my meaning and because I had been drinking beer for six straight hours, I said, "Whalebone," and then leaned over to kiss her collarbone again. Which was when she punched me smack in the face. As I was staggering around, yelling for someone to get me a napkin so I could stop my nose from bleeding all over myself, my beer, the bar floor, my sister-in-law called my wife from the bar pay phone and told her what I had done.

The next morning, I woke up on the living room couch where I had fallen asleep the night before. My wife was standing over me, holding a suitcase in her left hand.

"You're still drunk, aren't you?" she asked me.

"Yes," I said.

"Whalebone," she said, and then swung the suitcase and hit me square in the right ear, because this was not the first time I had woken up on the couch, still drunk in the morning; and it was not the first time I had kissed another woman in a bar; and it was not even the first time I had kissed my sister-in-law in a way that I shouldn't have. By the time my right ear stopped ringing, my wife had started the car and was on her way to stay with her sister.

I called my wife a few days later and tried to explain my actions in the bar. "I *imagined* I actually was kissing a whalebone," I told her. "I truly did."

"For someone who is so stupid," my wife said, "you sure have an active imagination." Then she told me she was leaving me for good, and hung up.

So here I am—no wife, no sister-in-law, no nothing—leaning over the woman my brother hit with the snowplow, and I ask myself: How does this look, me opening this woman's jacket and leaning over her the way I am? It looks bad, I know. The woman knows, too. Her eyes have narrowed into a squint, as if to say: "We might have a good thing going here. But I know men like you, always fucking up a good thing by moving too fast. So tell me: are you going to fuck this up?"

"No," I tell her. "I am going to do this *right.*" I zip up the woman's jacket and lie down in the snow next to her. I even take hold of her hand and she does not try to take it back, and I think I see her eyes widen a little bit.

We lie for there for quite a while. I admit to thinking some dramatic thoughts. You cannot lie down on top of a foot of virgin snow and look at the blazing blue sky while holding hands with a woman you are quickly and totally falling in love with, and not think of making a fresh start, of wiping the dirty slate of your past clean, of forgiving and forgetting. I start off by telling the woman that I forgive her for all the pain she has caused me in our brief time together. The only way in which she has caused me pain, of course, is that she won't let me know, definitively, whether she is dead or alive. But I tell her I don't care.

"It doesn't *matter* whether you're dead or alive," I tell her. "I'm *fine* with it."

She doesn't withdraw her hand or cough nervously, which encourages me to launch into a whole series of true confessions.

"You know the plow?" I ask her. "The one my brother hit you with? It's stolen." I tell her how my brother and I were in Ontario last January, and how we ended up in a bar, drinking with the rightful owner of the plow. He was a good old guy with a handlebar mustache who told us how he had somehow grown attached to the plow as if it were an actual human being, how he drove it everywhere in the winter, even to the bar itself. After a few hours of drinking with us, the old guy passed out. "We took the plow keys right out of his pocket," I tell her. "My brother drove the plow home, and I followed him in the car."

The woman narrows her eyes again. I know immediately that she doesn't believe me. We're like that, she and I, we know each other's thoughts. So I say, "It's true. The border guard waved us right through. It was freezing. They were waving everyone through. The other plow is mine, though, legitimate."

Then, before she can stop me, I say, "And my brother shouldn't even be driving the plow. It's no surprise he hit you, I could see it coming. He's a menace. But I don't pay him hardly anything and it makes me feel good,

screwing him that way. He lives with me, in my basement, and I charge
him too much rent and he *pays* it. That feels good, too. He's my older
brother and he teased me when we were kids, and I still hate him for it."

She doesn't say anything at all! The woman just lies there calmly,
circumspectly looking at the wide blue sky, as if to say: I understand
completely, tell me more, I want to hear everything. As if to say: If this is
going to work, then we mustn't hide anything from each other. And so I
tell her everything. I tell her about the time a beer buddy and me jumped
this smart, skinny guy out at a party on Sabin Road because he was too
damn smart and because he was too skinny to fight back much. We beat
on him a little until my beer buddy said: "Why are we doing this?"

I said, "Because he was talking bad about your sister," which I just
thought of on the spot.

"No he didn't," my buddy said. "I don't even *have* a sister." And so
the buddy and the skinny guy beat the hell out of *me*. But I don't tell
the woman this last part.

Instead, I go on and mention that time when I didn't go to my
father's funeral because my father had heard, months before he died,
that I had been running around on my wife. He'd confronted me about
it one Saturday morning, while we were out deer hunting.

" 'You will not keep on hurting that girl the way you are,' he said.

I said, " 'Mind your own business.'

" 'Unfortunately,' he said, 'you *are* my business.' " Then my father
poked me in the chest with his twelve gauge. Hard.

"It was humiliating," I tell the woman. "So I didn't go to my father's
funeral. Never been to his grave, either." I'm still holding the woman's
hand, but I don't look over at her because of what I'm about say next,
which is basically that my father was right: that I *did* run around on my
wife and that I *did* hurt her, bad, for all ten years we were together. I
give the woman the whole, sordid story: the cheating, the wrecked cars,
the money stolen from my wife's purse, the fantastic, sprawling lies. "I
am a vicious, immoral moron," I tell the woman. "That's a direct quote
from my wife." I don't spare my new love any little detail about the
complete piece of crud I was and mostly still am.

When I am finally done it feels like hours have passed. I look over at the woman, still lying next to me, still holding my hand. *I've blown it,* I think, because the woman's face is pale, very pale, and she is crying. The tears are positively streaming down her cheeks.

"Please don't," I say. I reach over to wipe away her tears and I find that they're not tears at all! It's merely that there was some snow on her forehead, and it is now melting in the sun. Now that I realize this, the woman appears to be in fact quite happy. She even looks to be smiling, the corners of her mouth rising slightly in playful disbelief, as if to say: "There must be more. Come on. You haven't done anything worse than *that?*"

"That's it," I say, getting happier and happier and deeper in love and deeper in love. I don't think I've ever been this content, not even when my brother and I were drinking beer this very morning, right before we took the plows out, which makes me remember one more thing I need to confess.

"I'm a drunk!" I tell her. "I'm drunk right now!"

The woman continues to smile. "Is that really it?" seems to be her response.

"It is," I tell her and then relax more completely into the snow, which is soft and melting in the sun and feels like wet foam rubber. Never in my life have I been so *whole.* I actually feel saved, religiously saved. "Where did you come from?" I ask her. "You're some kind of angel, aren't you?"

And then I wonder: Where did she come from? And then I think that she actually might *be* an angel, because the field we're lying in is in the absolute middle of nowhere. There are no houses nearby and there is no car anywhere that she might have driven here in. The idea that the woman is an angel suddenly makes utter, perfect sense: how would she have gotten here if she weren't? "Wow," I say, because it's disconcerting falling in love with an actual angel, because that means that you haven't chosen *her,* but that *you've* been chosen. And when you've been chosen by an angel, you must sit up straight and act nobly and do *good.*

I sit up straight with the thought of having to do good, and in doing so I see something sticking out of the snow a few feet away from us. I get up to investigate and I find one cross-country ski, then another one a few feet away.

So she is not an angel after all. She's a cross-country skier. I'm disappointed at first, understandably, but then I have this really fantastic idea. The Olympic Training Center at Lake Placid is not far away from here, and I know it's an Olympic year. It occurs to me that the woman is an Olympic skier and that she was out training for the 50K race or the Nordic Combined when my brother hit her with his plow.

I gather up the skis and trudge back to the woman. "You didn't tell me you were going to be in the Olympics," I say.

She still has that sly, modest smile frozen on her face. Clearly she didn't want to tell me, didn't want me to think she was showing off. Clearly she wanted to get to know me first before she confessed to being an Olympic athlete.

"I'm so proud of you," I say. "It's just wonderful." And it is. I can see our whole life in front of us. I will give up the plow and my sorry brother and our crappy hometown and my sordid, lonely life, and follow her to Squaw Valley, Oslo, Lilliehammer. I will wax her skis and get her lucrative endorsement deals and give her backrubs and menace her competitors if I have to. Then, once I have proven my devotion and my love, I will divorce my wife, marry this woman, and finally find some happiness in this world.

I am so excited by this idea that I am about ready to load this woman and her skis into my plow and begin our new life together when the sun hits me in the eyes, right in the eyes where it shouldn't this early in the morning, right smack in the middle of winter. Then I remember that it is not right smack in the middle of winter. It is the first week in April. And aren't the winter Olympics in February or something?

"Hold on a second," I say to the woman. I run over to my plow and get my brother on the CB.

"I'm already back at the garage," my brother says. "Where the hell are you?"

"You hit a woman," I say.

"Did not," he says.

"Nevermind," I say. "Listen. When are the winter Olympics this year?"

There *are* no winter Olympics this year, he tells me. "The summer Olympics are in Atlanta. They start in July."

"God*damn* it," I say. I slam the CB against the dashboard, because the woman has obviously lied to me about being an Olympic skier. She is not an Olympic skier at all; she is only an ordinary, amateur skier who was trying to cross the road when she shouldn't have. Here, I have shown her my true black heart, pledged myself to her, made big plans for us, and what do I get? I get lies. And if the woman has lied about being in the Olympics, then who knows what other lies she has told? Who knows what lies she might yet tell?

I am so angry that I come close to running over there and just letting her have it. I am no stranger to ugly breakups. I know how to make a woman miserable. I know how to ruin her name, her reputation. I know how to pour sugar in a woman's gas tank. I know how to do lots of things.

But I don't do any of this stuff because I am thinking clearly now, much more clearly than normal. It occurs to me that if this woman can so easily let loose with this big whopper of a lie, then who knows what kind of truly twisted stuff she might be capable of. You can never tell about people these days. I suddenly have a vision of us, ten years or so down the road from now. I am lying on the couch, and this woman is standing over me with a suitcase. And since she is a lunatic, an absolute sick *fuck,* then the suitcase is packed with rocks or cinder blocks and she is about to smash me in the ear with it, just like my wife. And you *know* I don't need *that* again.

This premonition changes my way of thinking completely, and I start backing away from the woman because—and this seems obvious to me now—I am absolutely afraid of her, just as I'm afraid of my father and my wife and her sister, just as I'm afraid of anyone in this world who doesn't take any *shit.* I am such a coward that I almost start running away.

But I don't run away. *Easy now,* I tell myself. *Just calm down,* because while it's imperative that I get rid of this woman, I certainly do not want to spook her in the process. I have been through a few court-ordered rage-management and alcohol-awareness seminars, and so I know a little something about trying to defuse potentially dangerous situations. I suck in a deep breath and take the long, generous view of this woman. True, she has lied to me. True, she doesn't deserve the affections of a man like me. But after all we did have something *special*, and I will not ruin the memory of our time together by being ugly now. I will dump her respectfully, like a gentleman. Then, once I have dumped the woman, I will get in my plow and head back to the garage. My brother will be there, drinking beer, and I will drink his beer and dock him a day's pay for ruining another plow blade.

Just the thought of me sticking it to my brother makes me feel very brave indeed. I even forget why I was scared of the woman in the first place. So I walk over to where she is lying in the snow. She is still smiling; she obviously still has high hopes for me and her, and it actually pains me when I tell her that it's over between us. But I know it's the right thing to do.

"Don't," I say before she can try to talk me out of it. "What we had was beautiful, but fleeting. Let us not have any illusions. We are in love now, but in ten years you would hate me."

Accidents

I was in the darkroom with my editor. It's Tuesday, May 29, the day my wife finally ended our marriage, and the day after one of my many accidents. My editor was busy developing pictures of a Memorial Day parade, a crumbling monument of a man and a horse, a small American flag sticking out of a Panama hat. The pictures were to be part of the afternoon special edition, which was entitled: "The Memorial Day Experience in Smalltown, U.S.A." My editor was whistling "I Walk the Line." He was truly loving those photographs.

"I'm really cooking with gas in here," he said.

"That's a good idea," I told him. Then I waited for him to offer me some of his bourbon, which we believed to be the true, stout heart of our great newspaper heritage. My editor and I are traditionalists: that is, we drink, just like the newsmen of yore. But at all else journalistic we are inadequate, grammar poor and not very proud, nor tough, and we are terrified of the hard-boiled and incapable of cutting to the chase. The chase here is that I waited until my editor finished developing his pictures, after which he gave me a drink of Old Granddad from his dinged-up aluminum flask. The bourbon tasted warm and a little metallic. I handed the flask back to my editor, and he drank and I watched him. There wasn't much of a human being left to look at.

"How do you stay so thin?" I asked him.

"Peas. All I eat is peas."

"Let's get a look at those teeth," I said. "Don't they turn your teeth all green, those peas?"

"You've got some funny ideas, my friend," he said, putting his hand on my shoulder. The flag waved at us from the developing bin and my editor waved back. My editor, Phil, has been in charge of the Herkimer (N.Y.) *Mountain Enquirer* for fifty-two years. He is eighty-five years old and truly proud of his age. When he hired me two years ago, Phil asked me what my goals were. I had no goals at all, but I lied and said that I wanted to help those who needed help, photograph both the triumphant and tragic, and win the general acclaim of the newspaper community. My editor said I was aiming too high. His was a success story, he said, because the only goal he'd ever had was to live to a reasonably old age. Phil then told me that he only hired people like himself, folks who couldn't do the job well, but could do it for a long time.

"Are you the kind of person we're looking for?" he asked me.

I told him I was, and used the phrases "long-term commitment" and "company man."

"Super," my editor said.

I started drinking with my editor that morning because of my wife. I drink with him most every morning, for pretty much any reason you can think of. But that morning my wife blew up at me on account of our car, which I had dragged home the night before all covered with chicken fat. I had parked it under an exhaust fan at the Kentucky Fried Chicken. It took five minutes all in all, which is an eternity in the tragic scheme of things.

"You put that car where you shouldn't have," Ellen said when she saw it slicked-up in the driveway.

"Correct," I told her. I had known about the exhaust fan. Everyone knows. It is the most common kind of knowledge.

"Tell me you did it out of spite, you awful bastard," she begged me. "I can't take one more accident in this world."

I couldn't lie to her. I told her I flat out forgot. Which really set her off. The chicken fat took on a marital weight that the old Colonel himself couldn't have imagined.

I dragged myself into work that next day on foot, and in a new state of regret.

"I need to be some kind of new man," I told my editor. He gave me another drink.

"That'll cure what ails you," he said.

"Yes," I said.

"That used to be a saying."

"It still is," I told him. Then he left to be an editor. It was ten-thirty in the morning and all the pictures were done except for the printing, and as the saying does not go, I felt very little of all right. I was all alone in the darkroom and still had to type up the farm report. There had been no good rain in the Adirondacks for two months, and all the severe Christian farmers were talking suicide and blue murder. I was afraid of what had to be said and that I was the one to say it.

I had for some time believed that my editor was homosexual, and the story of that belief is also the story of another accident. I came home one night four months ago and found my wife in bed, reading. I bent down, kissed her, and said, "El, the chief is a gay," and she looked at me in such a way that I couldn't tell who she was blaming and for what reasons.

"That's your opinion," she said.

This comment confused me. The words "duh" and "wha?" came to mind.

"Leon," she said, "Opinions are like assholes: everybody has one. Understand?"

"I guess so," I said.

"And this is the last time you'll share this opinion with anyone?"

"Sure," I said, wanting to make peace. "I promise."

El regarded me carefully, her sea-green eyes searching and flashing in the light of the bedside lamp. When I showed no sign of weakness or deceit, she smiled and kissed me sweetly on the cheek. It seemed like a marital crisis had been avoided.

Forty-eight hours later, I was in the Uptown Lounge, hiding from the kind of winter night that we in upstate New York are so famous for. I was shooting pool with three good citizens named Boomer, Flex, and Geeker, high school buddies of mine who had kept their high school nicknames, and who had also continued to drive Ford 4 x 4 trucks, work for the country road crew, and publicly mourn our morally suspect and light-hitting heroes, the New York Yankees. The night stretched on, and we generally behaved the way alcohol counselors and Hollywood road movies say men like us do. There was mention of the working man, Caribbean booze-cruises, and the alcohol content of Canadian beer. Boomer claimed we should heed the genius of classic rock lyrics, and ignore the refined scratch-and-sniff that is poetry. Geeker agreed, and argued that the crash and scream of Led Zeppelin compared favorably to the yawp of Mr. Walt Whitman, the whine of Mr. Eliot.

"Amen to that," Boomer said.

All this sound wisdom and fine human companionship left me feeling rich and untroubled. Around one in the morning I leaned over to someone—Flex, I believe—and told him my theory about my editor's sex life. After the story was told, I immediately felt less rich and more troubled, and I didn't know what made me tell it. To be true, I still don't know.

"Hot damn," Flex said, his big chest and shoulders doing a little dance inside his mesh New York Giants practice jersey. "Is it the truth?"

It took two days for the news to travel all the way through our town of five thousand beating hearts and loose lips, and then back to my wife.

"If I've heard the story," she said to me, "that means your editor has got wind of it, too, you know."

"It just slipped out."

"How could you?" she said.

"It was an accident," I said.

At this point, we'd been married a year and were loving each other for the usual reasons of trust and desire. We had gotten married because of love, but also because we wanted security and responsibility. El said that the physical attraction and clever talk that is new romance was good but volatile, and mostly temporary.

"I want something more and better," she said the night we were engaged.

I agreed and told her that marriage would be our stable thing in an unstable world.

During that first year, El endured misplaced income tax papers, knocked-over geranium pots, missed car payments, broken condoms, lost airplane tickets, and the like. Once, during a generous Thanksgiving dinner at El's parents' house, I held forth on the flag-burning controversy, on which I was a liberal. I had somehow forgotten that El's father was a veteran of two foreign wars; on his desk down at the Ford dealership, he showcased a picture of himself sitting on top of a Sherman tank. In the picture, as in real life, El's father sported a crew cut, a military scowl, and a good, straight spine. I acquired several nicknames that night, including "Uncle Fidel" and "King of the Pussies." El's father declared that I sucked all the joy out of his wife's creamed onions. "God," he said, "you make even the cranberry roll taste burnt."

I apologized for all these things by saying they were accidents, and El acted saintly and accepted the apologies. This one-sided give-and-take changed when I claimed my slip up about the chief was an accident: in fact, it was exactly at that moment that honesty became ugly, attraction became revulsion, and that El stopped wanting my male companionship. The problem was I still loved her and for a long while lobbied for my worthiness as a life-partner. Which made her hate me even more.

Eventually, we went to a marriage counselor, Dr. Purdy, who is now also among those El distrusts. El explained to him the terms of our general decline, beginning with my many failures and ending with my inability to anticipate those failures. When the counselor asked her to explain my behavior, El suggested mild alcoholism, a short attention span, and, in the case of my editor, simple meanness of spirit.

"I just don't think Leon wants to be a better person," she said.

In response, I explained to Dr. Purdy the physical details of my life as a professional—the overlong handshakes, dinner invitations, back slaps, and numerous other things which best remain under the hat of therapy. Dr. Purdy heard us out and then said: "I don't think he's gay. He's just old. That explains almost everything, you know. There's not a damn thing we can do about getting old."

El sat there clench-jawed. She was chewing on her resentment. But I thought I spied some wisdom therein and about.

"All these things I can't change," I told the counselor. "It's got so I can't stand it."

He nodded. El stood up. She's a tall woman, which is why she became a librarian at the elementary school. Those kids are so needy when it comes to getting their top-shelf books on the Erie Canal and those genius junior detective novels. El has a world of patience and a fantastic reach. But she could have been anything. I admired her as she unfolded herself, smoothed her long cotton dress and said: "You are both hateful. Morons, too." Then she left us sitting there with our hands on our knees and we sat and finally I got up, and there was no need for any watch-looking or throat-clearing and I did not beat my breast for being a small fool at the mercy of a larger power.

Our time was up.

I didn't plan for life to be this way, nigh thirty and unlovable and no sense of how I got here. Looking back, I realize I didn't plan almost anything.

And one thing I didn't plan on is settling: settling for a job I do not care about; for the destruction of a once-good marriage; for adult life in the small, static town of my youth; for the clichés of mediocrity and failure that come with small-town living. I didn't plan on settling for any of these things. But neither did I plan on not settling. On this I have heard two things: *Never settle* and *Sometimes you have to settle*. The problem is not that you don't know when to settle, but that you don't know when you already have.

Another thing I didn't plan on was being seventeen years old and hurtling toward the transplanted sweet home of Stafford Philpott. Stafford Philpott was the new girl in my high school. She was blonde, hailed from Tupelo, Mississippi, and said the words "Sir" and "Honey" and "Good Lord" with a lilting accent that nearly melted my inner core. Stafford moved to Herkimer right before my junior prom. There was always a beautiful new girl at these dances, someone who had no regard for longstanding high school romance, prom etiquette, or full-throttle puppy love; someone who always left the prom with her mystique intact, but with everyone else's sense of self-worth in ruins. I had heard around school that Stafford was, in fact, planning on going to the dance, and so history told me that she would break the back of my junior prom, but I did not expect to profit from the back-breaking. I expected to get drunk; I expected my date not to. She was scarily efficient and fair-minded in her sobriety. She expected that her fondness for hyperbole would make her a really fine real estate agent.

I planned on her trying to confiscate my car keys.

"You'll thank me in the morning," is what I expected her to say.

She did.

"He doesn't even want to see you in the morning," is what I did not expect Stafford Philpott to say to my date, but Stafford did the unexpected. She spoke the truth. At that point in history, the Herkimer Magician junior prom was not equipped for the truth. The prom went up in the flames of discord, but I was already gone.

It was when I was in the car, steaming full bore through that black night, that I finally planned on tearing one off with old Stafford Philpott.

I ended up settling for the torching of her rich father's horse barn instead.

What happened was that Stafford deposited me in the barn, and went to talk to her father, who was a lawyer or doctor or some such thing. I laid back on a bale of hay. I fell asleep with my cigarette, and woke to my own barn burning, set not out of greed, nor as a weapon of class warfare, nor even because the world had forgotten about valor. It was set because I just don't understand how tragedy works.

Stafford's father tore in with a horse blanket, and I walked out of the barn and stood with Stafford and waited for him. Finally he came out. The horse blanket was considerably diminished. The barn was smoking miserably. I extended my hand, which the father stared at and then deferred for all time. Then he looked at his daughter and said, "My love, your friend here is a lout."

"I already knew that," she told him.

Three years later, I was in Oswego, New York, descending the stairs of my sorry fraternity with a professor's daughter from Lexington, Virginia. At the foot of the stairs was a puddle of vomit, surrounded by four boys who *were* louts. They were looking at the puke and discussing the who, the why, and the what now. One of those louts was advising a smaller one that he better haul ass and find him a mop.

To prove I was no lout, I released this girl from the near South and soared Errol Flynn-like over the puddle. Errol Flynn was no puddle jumper. It goes without saying, I did not make it. I was lying back-down in the thick of it, my right hand bloodied from a broken bottle of beer, and unlike Romeo without the dignity of the suicide pact, when the girl leaned over me and said, "Leon, we are from different worlds."

"I already knew that," I told her.

But the truth is I didn't know. I never would have known if she hadn't told me herself. What I do know is that I promised my roommate I would buy him a new white Arrow shirt. That promise remains unfulfilled. Instead, I fled school for home and for a job as a reporter for which I had no qualifications and needed none, to a beautiful girl named El who woke slowly to the agony of all my dumb accidents, but with no less pain because of the speed.

The end of El's and my marriage started as someone else's disaster and then became our own.

When I got out of the darkroom, my editor was running around in circles looking furious. Everyone else was standing over at the window.

"Where's my camera?" he asked me. "What in the hell did you do with my camera?"

"You don't have a camera," I told him, which was the truth as I knew it.

"The hell I don't," he said. "The hell I don't have a camera." He sounded like he had reached the outer limits of agitation, and I am sorry to say that I stood and wondered what would happen if he just fell over and died right there. I also wondered if I would be the new editor if he did. None of this makes me feel good as a human. He did not die, and I did not become the editor, for which the news is likely a little better off. The only other thing I can tell you is that he worried around for that damn camera a minute more and then sat down and stared at his computer screen. It was blue.

"Here comes the ambulance," someone said at the window. I walked over.

Three floors down there was the ambulance that had just pulled in. There was also a Chevy Nova with its driver's-side door wide open and this poor man lying on his back, right there on Prospect Street. Then there were all these people standing around who had nothing to do with anything.

When I got outside the man was still lying there, and the car door remained open. The keys were in the ignition and there was a dinging sound hassling me from inside the car. I took the keys out of the ignition and put them on the front seat of the car. Then I walked over to the paramedics. They were standing in a circle, talking, which is exactly what most people will do when they could be out there saving lives.

"There is a man on the ground over there," I told them.

"The battery was dead," one of them said. "Terry forgot to charge it." He stared at another paramedic, who I took to be Terry.

"I did not," Terry said. "It was someone else."

"Anyway," said the first man, "that's why we're late. The battery."

"What's wrong with him?" I asked, pointing at the body on the street.

"Use your imagination," the first one said. "It looks like an accident. Maybe it was a heart attack."

I took another look at the car. Its right side was resting against a street light. I don't know how I could have missed it in the first place. My brain must have been pickled from an excess of alcohol and husbandly grief. There was a big dent in the fender and a headlight was laid out all over the sidewalk.

"Did the crash cause the heart attack or the reverse?" I wanted to know.

"Who are you?" Terry said.

I began to hate him because I knew I had asked a good question.

"You're some piece of work," I told him. "You and that asshole battery." He ignored me and went back to talking with the other paramedics.

When you are alone and feeling completely helpless, as I was at that moment, you must properly assess your situation if you are ever to feel less lonely, less helpless. So I assessed: there was me and there was the dead man. The dead man had nothing, but I at least had a camera. So I stepped back and started taking pictures of him. I took them for the dead man himself, for the living me, for El. I took them to prove I was a useful and reliable member of the conscious world. Plus, I was so happy to have hard evidence of an accident that was worse than my own. Taking those pictures, I gave that man a history and my own poor self a sense of purpose.

But someone grabbed me from behind before I could finish taking the whole roll. I turned around to see who it was. It was a man.

"What do you think you're doing?" the man asked me. I had never seen him before. He had light blonde hair and a red, brilliant face.

"Nothing," I said.

"Nothing," he said. "You were taking those pictures."

"Oh yes," I said.

"You can't take pictures like that. I don't care what kind of person you are."

I just stared at him the way people do when their outwardly neutral deed has been exposed for the selfish act that it is.

"What are you talking about?" I said.

"That was the mayor you were taking pictures of," he said.

"No it wasn't," I said, but I wasn't too damn sure. It's true, I had seen the mayor plenty, but you never know how death will change someone.

The red-faced man looked back at the dead man and then back at me. His eyes spoke of sorrow and desperation.

"O.K." he said. "It's not the mayor. It's my father."

He started crying right then. That's when I felt some control over the whole situation.

"I'm sorry," I told him. "Your father."

"You can't print those pictures," he said. "That's nothing that belongs in the paper."

"You're wrong," I said. "You can't tell me the mayor's dead and then tell me you're lying and then start asking me for favors. I can't give you any credit here."

"Who needs to see that stuff?" he asked, still crying. "There is nothing important about it." He had a point, I realize that. But still, it made me feel so good and so accomplished taking those pictures, and I wasn't going to just give up that good feeling. So I walked away from the man and his dead father, went inside, developed the pictures, and sent them down to layout. Then, I went home.

I told El the whole story, except for the last part, once I got home. She listened carefully like it might mean something. When I was done she looked at me and asked, "So what did you do?"

"What did I do," I said. "What's right is right. I gave him back the pictures of his father."

El didn't say anything. I'll bet that she didn't even search out those pictures in the paper the next day, didn't need to see the proof that my history of accident and disruption had become a present of intentional deceit. El sat there awhile and then she stood up and walked toward me. Would you believe me if I said I saw the ghosts of our lives and love begging and choking in the shrinking space between us? Would it help if I said that were there a pill against accidental evil, rank insecurity, and plain human weakness, I would take it without water or hesitation?

And would it be too much if I told you that El was a lesson in the strait and narrow, that her legs, walking toward me, cut through the air of my low intentions?

What I mean is that she slapped me across the face and I agreed with her.

We have since moved out but not on, as people are rumored to do. When I'm not working I sit around, watch TV, and wonder how people like El seem to know things that I, as an eyewitness, do not. I figure if they were there, then they could say something. I figure I should tell her so. On the news last night, there was a story about three teenage kids in Florida. Those kids went out, got a little drunk, and stole a couple of stop signs. Then they went home. Two hours later, an eighteen-wheeler rolled on through an intersection where one of those stop signs was not, and killed a different carload of slightly drunk Florida teenagers. The day after, everyone was sick and grieving over the dead kids, so they went and charged the sign stealers with murder.

Oh, those poor fucking sign stealers.

Is this fair? Those three kids go to bed thinking they've committed one small evil, and wake up to find that they've accidentally fallen into a larger one. Is this justice? Why is it that those kids get blamed for the accident and not the intent? Is this how the world is supposed to work? Late last night, I figured that if El hadn't heard this story, then she needed to. So I picked up the phone and called her.

"El," I said. "This is Leon."

"I don't believe you," she said. Then she hung up.

Specify
the Learners

I t is the first day of school and already, Mrs. Posely wants to make love to me. She tells me so as we file out of the classroom, on the way to recess. But Mrs. Posely also says that she feels horribly conflicted. For one, she is married; for another, I am a student in her sixth-grade class.

"There are clearly rules against such things," Mrs. Posely says. "Well-meaning rules, necessary rules."

"I understand," I tell her.

"But on the other hand," she says, "you *are* a fully grown man." Mrs. Posely leans into me and whispers that when she first walked into class, the sight of me bulging out of my little desk chair nearly sent her running to the school psychiatrist.

"I'm so conflicted," she says again.

"I understand," I say again. And I do. On the one hand, I am, as Mrs. Posely says, a fully grown man. I was once married, and have had the moderately exciting sexual history of a normal thirty-three-year-old American male. On the other hand, my being here at Monroe Street Elementary School is highly suspect; I know the principal is watching me

like a hawk. Besides, it's my third time around in sixth grade, and I can't
afford to screw up again.

Still, a man in my situation must be highly politic. So I tell Mrs.
Posely that I'm conflicted as well, but that we must control ourselves.
Think of the other students, I tell her. She nods competently. Of course,
she says. Of course. I smile and I ask her if she thinks we can make it out
to the playground without violating any school rules. She smirks, flips a
piece of her wavy blonde hair off of her forehead, and I feel this great
throb of regret. For an elementary school teacher, Mrs. Posely is very easy
on the eyes.

Out on the playground, my classmates ask me the inevitable question:
what am I, an adult, doing here as a student in their sixth-grade class?
I tell them that my parents were killed in a political bombing and that
I am now living in town with an elderly aunt. My fellow students have
seen people killed by political bombings on television, and if their
parents were killed in one then they, too, would be pawned off on their
elderly aunts, and so my classmates accept my explanation.

The truth, however, is a bit more complicated. The truth is that
upon reaching the age of thirty-three without any real accomplishment,
I set out to discover why it was so. After several months of searching, I
determined that my crappy job at the paper mill, my crumbling marriage, my nagging drinking problem, *everything*, could be attributed to
the fact that I failed sixth grade back in 1977. Of course, I repeated the
grade the next year and passed. But the damage had been done. During
the course of my investigation, I recalled the humiliation I felt because
of my failure; I recalled my parents' crushing disappointment; I recalled
how my ambivalence toward my education became outright antipathy.
My discovery encouraged me to dig deeper. I had some tests conducted
and found that I have and have always had the following learning disabilities: dyslexia, attention deficit disorder, aphasia, hyperactivity, and
some others that I have difficulty remembering.

After learning all this, I became outraged at how my disabilities had
been so callously ignored, and how I was denied the appropriate

miracle drugs that we hear so much about these days. So I hired a lawyer, and sued the Little Falls Central School District for negligence and emotional distress. The lawyer was good, and our case was strong, and so the school district panicked and tried to settle out of court.

"What do you want?" the school district's lawyer asked me.

"I want to start over," I said. "I want to be enrolled in sixth grade again."

The lawyer consulted the school board, who ultimately agreed to my demands, thus recommencing my education.

All goes well until two weeks into the semester, when I earn the affections of one of my classmates. We are in the middle of our Native American unit, and our in-class assignment is to build a miniature long house in the grand Mohawk style. I've done some basic carpentry in the past, and so I volunteer to do the more intricate detail work involving the particle board and the papier-mâché. My classmates are very appreciative; whatever reservations they might have had about me seem to have vanished. The boys in particular have made me one of their own, and a group of them make a big production of slapping me on the back before running off to the classroom computers, where they punch up the racier internet sites and fidget with their private parts.

So anyway, the long house is nearly completed, and I am inside, putting the finishing touches on the fake-woven roof when I feel a tug on my shoe. I look down and see Loreen Miller, a tall, pretty red-haired girl who chews gum the way a termite might chew wood. Loreen is sprawled out in the entrance of the long house, her denim overalls bunched up at her shoulders like parachute straps.

"What is it?" I ask her.

Loreen doesn't answer. She simply reaches forward and unties the laces on my left shoe, and then bugs her eyes at me brazenly.

"Hey," I say, and pull my foot back, and while I am doing so, she unties the other shoe, deftly slips it off my foot, throws it at me, and then withdraws from the long house. I am flattered and more than a little thrilled by the whole thing, especially by the experienced, adult way in which Loreen slipped off my shoe. But I will have to watch myself: one of the stipulations of my enrollment was that I was not to have any *inappropriate* relationships with my fellow students. The school board would not define *inappropriate*. I have a feeling they intend to define it after the fact, and at my expense.

I come to school early and find a textbook on Mrs. Posely's desk. The textbook's title is *Specify the Learners*. I open up to the first chapter and read: "Today's classroom is a diverse one, and a successful teacher must be careful to accommodate the strengths and weakness of all of his or her learners. But the teacher must be able to specify the learners, as well: all classrooms have 'special' students and 'normal' students, just as societies have 'special' citizens and 'normal' citizens, and the teacher must be able to distinguish one from the other and adjust his or her expectations accordingly."

The passage sends a familiar chill through me. In my previous tenure in sixth grade, I was labeled "special" because of my inability to pass the required tests or stand in line during the fire drill or keep my hands to myself. The tag stuck, and I continued to be "special" as I made my slow, dumb way all the way to the eleventh grade, which is when I quit school and got on at the paper mill. After working at the paper mill for fifteen years, sweeping pulp and cleaning out the machines, I topped out at six-fifty-an-hour and acquired a nagging, burning sensation in my throat that has deepened my voice permanently, and which still causes me to cough up blood when it gets cold. This is why I wanted to return to Monroe Street Elementary in the first place. I don't think I can live through another fifteen years sweeping pulp. I vow to be normal at all costs. Please, oh please, let me be normal.

Mrs. Posely has somehow learned about the long house incident between Loreen Miller and me, and she is furious. A week after the long house has been completed, she calls Loreen up to the board to complete a complicated long-division assignment. Loreen may be bold, but she is not much of a mathematician. Loreen is simply not up to the task, but

Mrs. Posely tells her to try it again, and will not let her sit down. Finally, Loreen throws down her chalk and runs back to her seat in tears. Mrs. Posely looks at me in triumph and keeps looking at me until I get her meaning, which seems to be: If I can't have you, no one will. Then, she calls me to the board to complete the problem and I do so easily—because the drugs I'm taking for my various disabilities are working wonders and I'm a much better student than I was twenty-one years ago. When I have successfully completed the problem, Mrs. Posely compliments me on my work, and I thank her for her compliment and I hear Loreen in her seat, still sniffling. A point has been made, but I'm not sure what that point might be or who has made it.

The adults are wary of me. The other teachers watch me suspiciously as I walk down the hall, and they do not greet me by name as they do the other students; nor do they slap me five or hug me if I'm feeling down. And my old friends seem to distrust me as well, as I discover when I am invited to John O'Brien's annual Columbus Day party. John is a longtime beer buddy of mine, but he's also the father of Liz, one of my classmates. When I get to his house I immediately sense a tension. I sense that John has invited me out of loyalty, but that he wishes I hadn't come. I drink four or five beers out of nervousness, and then, to loosen things up, I tell a mildly filthy joke about Little Red Riding Hood and the Big Bad Wolf and a sexually transmitted disease. It is a joke that John has heard before, I'm sure, but he gets very upset and sends Liz upstairs to her room, and then asks me to leave.

"I'm sorry, Thomas," he says, "but you're making me very fucking uncomfortable."

I tell John that I understand, and then I leave.

And I do understand. After all, the adults know what it is to be an adult, and they think they remember what it is to be a child. But which am I?

My fellow students are obsessed with Jesus, and about what he would do under a variety of circumstances. They even go so far as to wear

shirts, necklaces, baseball hats, bracelets that ask: *What Would Jesus Do?*
It is coming up on Halloween, and so the questions are seasonal: Would
Jesus dress up as a witch? The devil? An astronaut? Himself? Would he
allow his parents to check the candy apples for razor blades, or would
he trust the neighbors not to be homicidal perverts?

Since Jesus himself is not around, my classmates turn to me for
answers. They know that I am thirty-three, and they also know that
Jesus died at thirty-three, and so for them the age is holy with meaning.
We are in the cafeteria, eating lunch, and they are all asking me: What
would Jesus do for Halloween, Thomas? I should be honored that they
think so highly of me, but instead I get agitated because I know that
compared to my classmates I am old, old, old, and that Halloween is
dead to me now. I get so agitated that I almost tell them that Jesus
would shut the fuck up and drink his chocolate milk. But I don't. I get
hold of myself and say: "Halloween is more than a week away. I think
Jesus would worry about his math homework and think about
Halloween over the weekend."

This is the wrong answer, even though we do have math homework,
and even though my classmates are absolute morons at fractions. But
still, I sound like a certain *kind* of adult. As a group they turn away from
me in disgust, except for Bobby Miller, Loreen's twin brother, who is
sitting next to me and who hisses "You're going to hell, and I'm glad." I
sit there red-faced and remember Mrs. Posely's textbook: *"all classes have
'special' students and 'normal' students."* I make a mental note to buy the
proper religious gear and be more normal, until I see Bobby's sister,
Loreen, leering at me from the across the table. I am clearly something
of a rebel to her: I would be her James Dean if she knew who James
Dean was. She blows a large bubble, takes it out of her mouth intact,
and pops it with her tongue in an obscene way. I momentarily forget
about being normal, about Jesus and about what he would do.

Right after Halloween we get a surprise ice storm, and we are kept inside
for recess. So Mrs. Posely gives us an impromptu assignment. The theme
of the assignment is: Where do we see ourselves in ten years? After a few

minutes of furious scribbling, Liz O'Brien stands up and says that in ten years she will have a job as a television reporter, a spouse, two children, a four-wheel drive vehicle, and a three-floor townhouse in Hilton Head, South Carolina. As for the rest of us, this is exactly where we see ourselves in ten years, too.

Mrs. Posely has husband troubles. I catch her crying at her desk during Silent Sustained Reading hour. Despite the similarities in our ages, I get that horrible breathless feeling children get when adults grieve in public.

"What is it?" I ask her.

"It's my husband," she whispers, so as not to disturb the other students. She tells me that she'd suspected her husband had been cheating on her for some time now, because of the late hours he'd been keeping and the fantastic, obvious lies he'd been telling her. "So last night I confronted him," she tells me. "He told me that he'd been sleeping with a woman at work for a year now. He admitted everything."

"Everything?" I say.

"He told me I'd get over it," Mrs. Posely says, and then starts crying again, streams of tears silently carving up her cheeks.

"Please don't cry," I say. To ease Mrs. Posely's pain, I tell her about my ex-wife, Christine, about how our love had waxed and waned over the fifteen years of marriage, and how she reacted when I told her I was returning to sixth grade.

"What about your job?" she said. Christine was a payroll secretary at the paper mill, and so she was much concerned with the bottom line. "What are we going to do without that money?"

"I never made much money to begin with," I told her. This was true; in fact, my wife herself had complained many times about the size of my pay stub.

"Are you really going back to elementary school?" she asked me.

"You know it," I said.

"You are a self-deluded idiot," she said, and then left me the next day.

"I'm so sorry," Mrs. Posely says. She puts her hand on my arm, and leaves it there for an overlong time. There is real heat in her touch.

Throughout the rest of the day, Mrs. Posely looks at me under heavy eyelids. The other students notice: someone coughs an obscenity, and I am kicked under my chair more than once by Loreen Miller, who sits behind me and who is clearly jealous. But still, Mrs. Posely scalds me with her stares. I suspect that I will not be able to hold her off for much longer. If there is anything a victimized woman loves more than a victimized man, I don't what it is.

I am becoming disillusioned with my education. I once believed that the world of learning was the antithesis of the world of manual labor. But I have noticed recently that the drudgery of the mill is not so estranged from the drudgery of verb conjugation or times tables. In both cases we are told that the drudgery is good for us, and in both cases we choose to believe what we're told. At the mill, we were given a fifteen-minute cigarette break if we were productive; in class, if we are good, Mrs. Posely reads to us out of some sickly sweet children's book. In both cases, we are told that this is adequate compensation for our excellence. We choose to believe this, too.

Right before Thanksgiving, I am called into the principal's office. The principal, Dr. Hudson, is standing over his desk, holding a sheet of paper, and when I enter his office, he hands it to me.

"Do you know what a petition is?" he asks me.

"Yessir," I say. Dr. Hudson is widely feared at Monroe Street Elementary School. Why, I am not sure. For one, he is a slight man, smaller than me, and not much bigger than some of my classmates. For another, he is pathologically dull: his good citizen speeches during assembly work like anesthesia on teachers and students, both. But for reasons that are not at all clear to me, we all are petrified of him.

"That document in your hands is a petition from the Parents' Committee," Dr. Hudson says.

"O.K."

"It is a petition to have you expelled," he says.

This gets my attention. I look at the piece of paper. At the top, it says something to the effect that I, Thomas Carney, have brought perversion into Monroe Street Elementary School, and that I should be expelled immediately. Beneath, there are a hundred or so signatures, a blur of blue and black ink cursive.

"I've done nothing wrong," I say.

"That's not what the petition indicates," Dr. Hudson says, and then taps the piece of paper with his index finger. I look at the petition again and see the signature of my buddy, John O'Brien, at the top. I remember telling John that dirty joke at his party, and I know immediately what has happened. I imagine John waking up the next morning after the party: he sits down to eat breakfast with his daughter, Liz, and remembers the joke I told him and then remembers that I am his daughter's classmate. What goes on in that classroom, exactly? he wonders. Does Thomas tell these kinds of jokes to my Liz? And what the hell *else* does Thomas do? My buddy John goes a little insane at the thought of me polluting his daughter and her education. So he riles up the other parents and starts a petition.

I don't tell Dr. Hudson, but it's true that I have told a dirty joke or two in class; and it is also true that I have thought, briefly, of Loreen Miller in a way that is perhaps inappropriate. But have I really done something all that wrong? I have not, and I tell the principal as much.

"Maybe not yet," he says. Dr. Hudson sounds disappointed; I know that he lobbied hard against my enrollment in the first place. He, too, must believe that I am something of a pervert. But it is important that he believe I am not a pervert; it is important that he know I am a dedicated student; it is important that I not have to go back to that paper mill. So I compose myself, and then ask: "How am I doing, Dr. Hudson?"

"How are you doing?"

"In class," I say. "How are my grades? Am I doing O.K.?" I know perfectly well that my grades are excellent, but I want the principal to tell me so. I want some official recognition of my success. But I do not get it.

"You better watch yourself, Mr. Carney," Dr. Hudson says. He flicks his bony hand at the door, and I leave.

· · ·

My classmates begin to hate me in earnest. It is early December, and we are studying local history. My classmates, for some reason, are restless: they refuse to learn the difference between the Battle of Fort Ticonderoga and the Surrender at Fort Stanwyck. But even when I was a bad student twenty-one years ago, I was adequate at local history. I am an absolute wiz at it now. I answer all of Mrs. Posely's questions about the Erie Canal, and I give a thorough, masterful report on the local branch of the underground railroad. Mrs. Posely gushes over my excellence in front of the whole class, and Loreen Miller slips me a note, saying I smell worse than stink itself, which I know means the opposite. But everyone else hates me for my success. I am ostracized in the lunchroom. I am heckled during art class for my watercolors. Finally, some of the boys jump me out on the playground. I don't even fight back. I simply let them hit me. But unfortunately for them, it is a cold day: the boys have mittens on, and I have on a heavy ski jacket, and so the blows don't wound me much. After a few minutes, the boys get frustrated, and run crying to Mrs. Posely. She placates them, all the while giving me sympathetic looks over their shoulders. But Mrs. Posely's sympathy is not enough. I don't know that I have ever felt this desperate. I think of sabotaging my grades to ingratiate myself; I think of offering to buy my classmates cigarettes, which I know they are hungry for. But it all seems so hopeless. Still, lacking any other option, I decide to stay the course.

We learn to see inadequacy as hope. Mrs. Posely tells me that she's had it, and is finally divorcing her husband. Her marriage has failed miserably, obviously, but I can tell by Mrs. Posely's increased interest in me that she has high hopes that she and I will not fail. Loreen can tell that Mrs. Posely, as a full-grown adult, has something that Loreen herself does not. But with this knowledge, Loreen has become even more juvenile in her affections: she sticks her tongue out at me with greater frequency, and her notes are more vicious than ever. And I get a phone call from my ex-wife, Christine. She says she has come to believe that our marriage was a tremendous mistake, and that it is all her fault. Christine says she mistook me for someone I was not.

"What's that?" I ask her.

"I knew you would be awful to me, but I thought you would at least be *exciting*," Christine says. "But you were not exciting. You were dull." Then, before she hangs up, Christine says that I shouldn't feel insulted, but that she's found a man who makes me look like the piece of furniture that I was and always will be.

And truth be told, I'm not insulted. I know exactly what she means. I failed sixth grade once and ruined my life, but this time I will pass sixth grade and my life will be different. We are inadequate once, and therefore believe that we cannot possibly be inadequate again. This is what I have learned during my time here.

On the heels of their petition, the Parents' Committee starts picketing the school. I arrive at school in the morning in mid-December, and I find thirty or so parents marching in a ragged circle in front of the school. They are holding large placards that read *School: For The Children* and *Parents Against Perverts*. When they see me, the parents curse at me viciously, and a baggy-eyed woman in sensible shoes even throws a cup of coffee at me, hitting me square in the chest. I nearly lose it and throw my backpack at her, but then I see Dr. Hudson watching from his office window, waiting for me to slip up. So I swallow my pride and go blot my jacket with paper towels in the boys' room.

Back in the classroom, the students seem unaffected by their parents' protest, despite their continuing disdain for me. During Mrs. Posely's basic chemistry lesson, they drift slowly from moderate interest to outright boredom. During their free time, they poke and push and provoke each other in the most suggestive ways. They are children in height and weight, but adult in world view and needs. This is what the parents fail to understand. They think that the difference between myself and their children is my experience and the children's innocence. The parents do not see that there are simply twenty-seven human beings longing to be released from our desk chairs, all of us desperate to be wanted.

. . .

The inevitable happens. It is the Monday before the school Christmas pageant, and so as a class we go to decorate the auditorium. I do my part, hanging the garland and stringing the popcorn along with everyone else, until Mrs. Posely calls from backstage, asking me to help her fix the manger. When I go backstage, Mrs. Posely is standing next to the rickety manger, a hammer in her hand, a lovely, self-deprecating look on her face, and the months of loneliness—the petitions, the parent protests, the classroom isolation—wash over me. I grab Mrs. Posely, and kiss her full on the mouth. She drops her hammer, kisses me back, and then abruptly pulls away. "Not here," she whispers. We agree to meet later that night at her house, and I, fully flushed with desire, go back to hanging garland.

It seems as if Mrs. Posely's and my embrace has gone unnoticed until a little while later, when Bobby Miller comes up behind me and makes a series of seductive revving sounds. *Vavoom*, he says. *Vavoom.* This is not definitive proof of anything: Bobby is obsessed with NASCAR, and is a seasoned participant in the Ford vs. Chevy debates that rage in our class-room. He has made these revving sounds before. But Bobby's face is inscrutable; it is impossible to tell what he knows and what he does not.

I meet Mrs. Posely at her house. She has bought plenty of red wine, and the lights are dim enough and her choice in music isn't terribly bad. It is a stimulating learning environment and my lesson proceeds as expected.

We are caught. I come to school on Wednesday morning and the first person I see is Loreen Miller. She sticks her tongue out at me, but sadly, halfheartedly, and this makes me nervous. I walk past her, into the school. Mrs. Posely is waiting for me outside the classroom. Her face is a quilt of splotches, and her voice is ragged: she clearly has been crying. She says that Dr. Hudson wants to see us, pronto. So we head to the principal's office. Dr. Hudson asks us to come in, closes the door behind us, and then tells us point blank that he's heard rumors about the two of us. I know immediately that Bobby Miller *did* see us backstage, and that he has told all there is to tell. Dr. Hudson wants us to confirm the rumors or deny them. I don't say anything. I figure I will simply keep my mouth shut and hope for the best. But Dr. Hudson is persistent, and finally Mrs. Posely breaks down and admits everything.

I am sent out into the hall to contemplate my fate while Mr. Hudson has a confidential discussion with Mrs. Posely. My thoughts are grim. I think about the glee of the Parents' Committee once they hear of my expulsion; I think about the inevitable, lurid local newspaper headlines; I think of my dingy, lonely apartment on Albany Street, and about my ex-wife in the arms of another man; I think about going back to the paper mill; I think about how in ten years I will not have the children I wanted, a four-wheel drive vehicle, a townhouse in Hilton Head.

After a few minutes, Mrs. Posely tears out of the principal's office without even looking at me. The principal ushers me inside. Strangely, Dr. Hudson is extremely solicitous. "Are you all right?" he asks. "Do you need to talk to someone?" and so on, until finally it occurs to me that he considers me the victim here, and Mrs. Posely the lecher. It is not clear whether Mrs. Posely has taken the fall for me, or whether Dr. Hudson simply believes in cases like these, that the student is always victimized by the teacher. But in any case, it appears that I will not be expelled. I am so relieved that I start crying. This only furthers the impression that I have been seriously wronged.

"Don't worry, Robert," Dr. Hudson says. "Everything will be just fine." As my crying comes to a shuddering stop, he puts his hand on my shoulder and tells me that all of this could have been avoided. He says that I should never have been put in that class in the first place, that I belong in a class for students with special needs. And I stand there, sniffling and nodding and full of hope, grateful that I've been given one more chance to succeed. Besides, what other choice do I have except to believe that Dr. Hudson knows what's best for me? True, once again things have not worked out for me in the regular class. True, I was labeled *special* once, long ago, and failed in life because of it. But the world has changed, and surely I will be better suited for the special class this time around.

The Reasons

M r. Millingford stands against the bookcase making sucking noises with his tongue and his cheeks.

"I always thought you were a drunk," I tell him. I have heard that this is the case. It is a well-loved story around school that Mr. Millingford passes out in the back seat of his Chevy Nova each Friday by midnight. The rumor maintains that large crowds gather to watch our librarian turn the glass of his car windows into a dense, bewitching fog, the steam of alcohol battling against night's unrelenting and oppositional cold as he sleeps it off.

"Yessir," I go on. "I was convinced you were the most obvious drunk around."

"I am a drunk," he says, his voice barely audible over the sound of his mouth preying upon itself. "I wish I were drunk right now."

"So it's all true then?" I ask, trying not to sound too surprised. "Every Friday. In your car."

"Yes," Mr. Millingford says. "All of it's true. There is even more, if you'd like to hear it."

"That's just great," I say. "It's nice to know you can count on something."

For the last four years I have believed in Mr. Millingford's inebriation like a novice priest longing for the truth of God, a desire that dares not have faith in itself but rather strives to trick belief into actual existence. Mr. Millingford's mythic alcoholism has always had great meaning for me, has always given my schooling some immediate sense of purpose. A routine. I feel a daily need to remind him of all his alleged problems. For instance, it is my habit to skip study hall with my friends just to tell Mr. Millingford every morning that he looks tired. We like to ask if he has been out late the night before, boozing it up with all the drunks we know or pretend to know or people we think have the potential to be drunks. My friends and I enjoy naming names, even if we have to make them up. We even form drinking motions with our pinky fingers and thumbs cocked, lifted, spoutlike, articulating gurgling sounds in our throats, as if we've been shot and are busy swallowing our own blood.

Mr. Millingford never says a word. He gives us a look that says he wants to slap us, knock our teeth loose and pick them up and store them in a box with overdue notices and misplaced file cards and other signs of abused property. But he never does. He straightens his glasses and goes about his awful, encyclopedic work with a patience that suggests there is a greater purpose to all things.

Now I know that he is in fact a drunk. That information turns out to be more insignificant than I could have imagined. This saddens me and then doesn't. The things that should matter don't. There, I know it. I am now that much smarter.

"You're always waiting," I tell him. "What are you always waiting for?"

He shrugs, a movement full of apology. But I already know. I know Mr. Millingford has been waiting for that moment when I finally get what's coming to me. Well, I've got it. What I do with it now is the issue of the moment.

"Where did you get that gun?" he asks.

"It's a .38," I tell him.

"But where did you get it?"

"At the gittin' place."

"That sounds familiar," he says. "I know that phrase."

"Mrs. Caprice," I say. "Senior honors English."

He nods, his head moving like some fatalistic, wrong-way metronome. "Flannery O'Connor. *A Good Man is Hard to Find.* PS 347. O 33." The librarian recites the call numbers sadly, as if his general knowledge confirms his own helplessness.

"No, that's not it," I tell him. "You aren't as smart as I thought. To be honest, I can't remember exactly where it's from. I do remember, though, that the boy who said it killed three men before he was killed himself. He didn't mind dying, although I'm sure the men he killed did. There was a big deal made over their suffering. I remember that much."

"Are you sure this is what you want?" Mr. Millingford asks. He moves forward slowly, pulling his reasonable-adult routine.

"None of that," I say, waving my gun like it's some bony, Ichabod Crane index finger in full scold. Mr. Millingford beats a quick two-step back to the bookshelf.

"You're a tough kid, aren't you?" he says, a world-class suck-up.

"I *am* a tough kid," I tell him. "I also have a horrible life at home. You know what that means, don't you? Good kids, bad environments."

This said, I cock my hip and try to look like a killer, and he strikes and maintains a slouch, looking like a victimized still life, and we stand there.

Mr. Millingford's mouth keeps pulling and pushing on its various parts, drawing and exhaling loudly as if it is trying to resuscitate itself. I have never seen him do this before today. I have never seen anyone do it. It must be a nervous habit that comes with the threat of death or the promise of certain types of large-scale change. It is not a comforting thing to watch.

I find myself pulling my own cheeks inward with my tongue and then I stop.

Finally, I waggle my gun at him. He stops his breathing exercises and puts his arms up without me telling him to. His cheap shirt is stuck to his skin, a translucent cotton-blend sealskin. The shirt looks like it was manufactured wet, more a texture than a color or a condition. I wave the gun again, and he puts his arms down, as if there is a string between him and me and I am pulling it.

"But you're not only a drunk," I say. "What else are you?"

"I'm a librarian," he says, not without pride.

"Yes, you are a librarian. And you're something else, too. You're at least one more thing."

We stare at each other for a long time. Mr. Millingford looks at the gun and I look at his hair, which is blonde, retreating in double time over his forehead. He looks at my white basketball sneakers, and I look through the window behind him, into the hallway. It is empty because of the fire alarm I've just pulled, and I know that it won't be that way for much longer. He looks at the red dye on my hands from where I grabbed the alarm, looks at the red transferred from my hand to the gun's grip, and I stare him in the eyes, willing him to do the same. Mr. Millingford finally raises his eyes, all vague and teary and nearly unable to focus, and through our looks we come to the understanding that I will shoot him if he doesn't tell me at least one more thing about himself, and it is possible that I will shoot him anyway.

"I'm your mother's boyfriend," Mr. Millingford says finally. The heels of his wing-tip shoes click nervously against the blue spine of the *World Book: A–H* on the bottom shelf.

"'My mother's boyfriend,'" I repeat. "That's an interesting way of putting it, especially since my mother is married to my father. Technically, then, I'm not sure you can be my mother's boyfriend. Her lover, maybe. Does that sound better to you? Lover?"

"That sounds fine," he says.

"She's very pretty, isn't she?" I ask him.

"Yes," he says.

"Much better looking than you are. Wouldn't you say that? You wouldn't say you were better looking than she is, would you?"

"I'm not sure what difference that makes," he says, not all the pride sucked out of him yet. "This is a very strange conversation."

"That's not what I'm asking you."

"No," he says. "It's not even close. She's very beautiful."

"I'm just trying to understand," I tell him.

He nods slowly, like he knows his head might pop off at any moment, that his spine is a thin, frayed chord. "I realize that," he says.

"I saw you the other night," I say. "I saw you outside the bar, the two of you in your car. I bet you're a shitty kisser. That's the one thing I could tell from where I was standing across the street. Your mouth is all wrong. It's like it isn't even attached to your face, like it is somebody else's mouth and you can't control it."

This is an insult he can't swallow. There is always something.

"I saw you there," he tells me, the sweat pouring out of his scalp now, down the thin, flat sides of his face and into the corners of his mouth. I watch as Mr. Millingford's mealy yap attempts a grin through his body's own deluge. "I saw you looking at us."

"I know you did," I tell him and then I shoot him in the left ankle, right where there is bone and tendon and not much else. Nothing that he really needs to live. Mr. Millingford falls to the ground, and his mouth takes on a crazy O-shape, like he's preparing to swallow the world. Then out of it comes a fierce rumbling noise, like he's a cow giving birth and dying at the same time. This goes on. I wait for him to stop yelling at me, at his own disabled foot, for him to get accustomed to the pain before I make him get up again. There is a quiet in the library, something in and around us that has made me deaf to the sound of the gunshot, of the fire alarm ringing, of Mr. Millingford bellowing even though I know they are all real, all things that I am directly responsible for.

"I have shot him," I think, wondering what else I might be now capable of. My school motto says: "There are no impossibilities, only weak imaginations."

Mr. Millingford stops yelling. He is trying to act like a quick healer, someone tough on the inside, and who knows, maybe he actually is. The librarian makes a move to get back on his feet. I tell him to grab onto the bookcase for support, and he does, holding it like it is the mast of a wounded sailboat.

"When you were in the car," I tell him, "you looked like you were enjoying me being there. You looked like you never wanted me to leave."

"I was enjoying myself," Mr. Millingford says. He voice is thick, ragged, like his teeth have embedded themselves in his tongue and in his throat. "I was happy you were there to see it."

"How happy?" I ask him. He looks down at his foot and sees that there is blood on the carpet and on the *World Book: A–H.* The blood drips cautiously and steadily out of his body like water from some snowpile caught out of season. He looks back at me. Mr. Millingford knows I am not a bad kid, despite my having shot him, and he guesses that there are ways out of this that even I can't see. He closes his eyes and tries to think of them. He wonders about all the right things to say. He imagines himself limping away from all this. I know that's what Mr. Millingford is thinking because his good leg shakes like there is a bee caught inside his pants.

"Not that happy, in retrospect," he finally admits. In this case, lying is the best policy.

"That makes sense," I answer. "It seems like the logical thing to say. I think we're going places."

"I hope so," he says. "I really hope so."

"There is just one thing I want to know before we go on," I say, switching the gun to my left hand so I can give my right hand a rest. My wrist hurts from the tightness of my grip, throbs like it is another heart, but I don't rub it.

"I can't help thinking about my parents," I explain. "My parents are on my mind. They locked themselves in their bedroom last night, killing each other for five hours straight. It seems like a relevant term, 'killing themselves.' They were pretty quiet about the whole thing, considering. I stood outside and listened to them talk. Not yell, but talk about how things go wrong, who was at fault, what could have been done differently. They talked like we're talking. Calmly. Under control. They decided that they couldn't have done anything at all, couldn't come up with one thing they might have changed if they had the chance. Not one damn thing. Can you imagine that? My mother called my father a fatalist, and he said that she was one to talk, and they both agreed with what the other had said. It was finished like that. But I could tell. I could tell that they were dying. There were breaking sounds coming out of their mouths, if that makes any sense. I don't expect you to know. But there is just one thing I need to understand."

"What is it?" Mr. Millingford asks. He seems attentive. He wants me to know that he will help me if he can. That is his job, after all.

"I need to know why. I know what you did and what my mother did and I know where you did it. Now I need to know why you did it. And even better, I need to know why my mother did it."

Mr. Millingford falls back against the bookcase, as if I have shot him again and he knows that he is dead already.

"You want reasons," he says, his librarian's voice quietly pleading with me to tell him that he has misunderstood, that I want something else entirely. But Mr. Millingford's powers of interpretation are just fine. I nod and we stand there while the school refills and crowds against the doors of the library, and we stand there still like two poorly made statues in full combat, cracking and crumbling in full view of each other as we wait for what comes next, the part that might tell us about all the things we can't know and how there is nothing in them for us to learn.

Up
North

I was working as a newspaper reporter up north in Little Falls, New York—the town where I had lived all my life—when the Urbanski Brothers' Circus and Wild Animal Show visited town. On the day the circus opened, I walked around and took pictures of the animals and the carnies, and interviewed some of the audience members and the circus performers. I learned that the trapeze artists and human cannonballs, who were supposed to be Romanian gypsies, were actually illegal Cubans and legal, but disgruntled Puerto Ricans. The Puerto Ricans had designs on illegality and were jealous of the Cubans, who they thought flew a little farther out of the cannon and a bit higher off the trapeze. The Cubans and Puerto Ricans attempted to speak English with Eastern European accents, and when they did so they sounded French, but the people in the audience thought they were either Germans or Jews. The audience members were themselves both Catholic and American, which left them fairly sure of their own identity and very unsure about whether these visiting daredevils were disgusting or inspirational. One thing they were absolutely sure about were the circus dwarves, who were from

Florida and Texas and who spoke with their own Southern accents. Little Falls had just lost its only paper mill to Mississippi, which had offered the mill owners lenient environmental laws and the usual Southern hospitality. The mill itself was a noxious, rotting husk which polluted your line of vision along the already considerably polluted Mohawk River, but the unemployed workers thought the mill and the river extraordinarily beautiful. The ex-mill workers stared murderously at the dwarves and wondered what other objects of beauty Mississippi might steal from them. On the ringmaster the audience was liberal and had no opinions.

During the opening ceremony, while the dwarves whizzed around on their motorcycles and the clowns wrestled with the yoke of comic relief, a little boy sneaked into the elephant tent and spooked a great African elephant named Whitney, who of course crushed the boy and went on a rampage, until he was tranquilized by his trainers. The boy, who was seven, had been warned not to go into the tent by his father, who was in the stands glaring at the midgets when his son was crushed. The boy had also been warned the day before not to punch his sister in her left ear with his right fist; not to throw golf balls at passing cars; not to refer to his teacher as "Stench" because of her unrelenting halitosis. The boy was also encouraged not to be a hateful child, which he was but might not have been eventually. The elephant Whitney was generally well-liked and had no enemies.

When the crowd found out about the boy, they listened carefully to their own considerable dramatic inclinations. They went out and found a crane, and brought the crane back to the Veterans' Memorial Field, where the circus was being held. They forced the elephant's trainers to calm Whitney while they slipped a chain around his neck. Once the chain was in place, the rest of the circus performers and personnel were run out of town. The crowd then hoisted Whitney up with the crane and hanged him. Later, they dumped the carcass in the river, and then went to bed.

The day after the town had hanged Whitney, the emotional pitch was still so high that they decided to hold a funeral procession for the dead little boy. The funeral director in charge of the procession organized it to look like something he thought you might see in Kenya or Thailand or New Orleans. The high school marching band brought up the rear of the procession and played patriotic songs and "Pomp and Circumstance." Many of the people in front of the band held up home-made felt banners, decorated with photographs of the dead boy and sequined outlines of the hanged elephant. The dead boy's father and five other men marched slowly at the head of the procession with the boy's casket on their shoulders. The procession moved up Loomis Street, past Ho Ho's Chinese restaurant and the Shear Ego hair salon, then took a left on Main Street, past Aiello's News, and the Stitch 'n' Time yarn shop, which was having its latest in a long line of going-out-of-business sales. Soon, the funeral procession reached the series of bars that lined the west end of Main Street—the Geegaw Lounge, the Happen Inn, the Renaissance, the Full Moon Saloon. Most of the men remembered and spoke of the many adult hours that they had sat in those bars and suffered that sinking, bad feeling that comes from lack of worldly accomplishment; most of the women talked about how much they hated both the bars and the thought of what their husbands did in them. But both the men and the women noticed how different they felt walking past those same bars along with the rest of the procession. By this point, everyone had forgotten all the small evils the dead boy had committed and were very sorry that he had died; but they were glad that they had so quickly avenged his death, and they congratulated each other on doing such a fine, brave job of hanging the elephant.

The procession took a right on Furnace Street and walked up a hill, stopping eventually at the Sacred Heart Catholic Cemetery. The people then grew quiet while the town mayor stood up and made a speech. He reminded them of the last time Little Falls had held a hanging. It was in 1893, he told them, when an Iroquois Indian field hand named Miller pushed his boss off the top of a barn. The Iroquois was angry over the money the boss owed him in the specific, and over his bad cultural history in general. The town took the Indian and hanged him from the nearest elm tree, which years after started dying out to Dutch elm disease. The mayor remarked on how it was now easier to find a crane than an elm tree, and how it was also easier to hang an elephant than a human being.

Then the mayor asked for complete silence. He held the hand of the dead boy's father, who was a big, bearded man and who wept softly while a priest prayed for the boy's eternal soul. When the priest was finished, the boy was buried.

The next year, the town held a celebration on the anniversary of the elephant's hanging. The chamber of commerce made up T-shirts that read: "Little Falls: The Town that Hanged an Elephant." The local paint store donated several gallons of gray paint, and the lumber company donated plywood and leftover two-by-fours. Various citizens took the materials, and conspired to create a crude, but life-sized wooden elephant. Then they dragged the crane onto Veterans' Memorial Field, and hanged the gray wooden elephant against the dark green backdrop of the nearby Adirondack Mountains.

The sight of the wooden elephant swinging in the spring breeze from the crane made everybody feel nostalgic and community-minded, including the dead boy's father. The father cried everyday over his poor dead son and was even leaking grief at that very moment, but the sight of the elephant cheered him up considerably, as did all of his neighbors, who comforted him with stories of his boy's fine, enduring qualities. I had been to high school with the father, and was waiting around so I, too, could praise his dead son. When his neighbors left, I put my hand on the father's shoulder. He turned to face me.

"That's something beautiful to see, isn't it?" he said to me, pointing at the elephant.

As I said earlier, I was born in Little Falls, had lived there for thirty-one years, and was accepted as a true, native part of the community. But some time before the elephant had crushed the boy, I began to feel that I was completely alone, even though I knew nearly every human in the town and had loved and hated many of them. I had loved and hated one of them so deeply that I had married her, and was then divorced by her for many of the same reasons other women in town divorced their husbands. I often saw her around town with her mother and father, whom she lived with and whom I also loved and hated, and when I saw them I felt even more lonely. It bothered me to feel so isolated amidst all these people I knew so well, and so I decided to coldly and objectively find out why it was so. As part of my job, I covered peewee basketball games, zoning-board meetings, and high school proms, and I learned all the thoughts and fears and wants of the people in the town. I took pictures of new hospitals, train wrecks, V.F.W. initiation ceremonies, and grange picnics, but none of those things made me feel any less alone, and none of them were beautiful. This alienation still terrified me, but it also made me feel a little superior. But when I squinted up at the wooden elephant swinging in the breeze—with its warped baseboard for a trunk and whittled birch branch for a tail—and I thought of all it represented, something melted within me. I turned to the dead boy's father, and found that I could no more look at him coldly and objectively than I could myself. I again stared at the elephant, way above our heads, some-where between ourselves and God, and there was no question that I felt less alone, and that I did find the wooden elephant beautiful. So I turned to the father, whom I was by now very afraid of, and said, "What?"

"Thank God for that elephant!" he said, raising his voice. "Do you understand me when I tell you that?"

The Author

Brock Clarke is from upstate New York. He received his Ph.D. in English at the University of Rochester, and is currently an assistant professor of English and Creative Writing at The University of Cincinnati. His fiction and nonfiction have appeared in *New England Review, Mississippi Review, American Fiction, The Journal, Brooklyn Review, South Carolina Review, Chronicle of Higher Education, Twentieth Century Literature,* and *Southwestern American Literature.* He has received awards from the Sewanee Writers' Conference, Bread Loaf Writers' Conference, and the New York State Writers' Institute. He lives with his wife, Lane, and their son Quinn in Cincinnati, Ohio.

Lane W. Clarke